ISN'T IT ABOUT TIME?

The place is Richmond, a suburb south-west of London. And something terrible—or wonderful—has happened. An English scientist, known only as the Time Traveler, has invented a machine....

THE TIMELESS MACHINE

MARK MALAMUD

after H. G. Wells

for Jasper Finn

THE TIMELESS MACHINE

© 2020 by Mark Malamud
Cover Art © 2020 by Veronica Mortellaro

First Regulus Press Printing May 2020
Signal Library 10-0202-21-50

Regulus Press, Seattle, WA
www.regulus.press

The Timeless Machine includes passages from *The Time Machine* by H. G. Wells, published in 1895 and in the public domain.

ISBN: 0999446270
ISBN-13: 978-0-9994462-7-0
(Regulus Press)

With relief, with humiliation, with terror, he understood....

— Jorge Luis Borges, "The Circular Ruins"

CONTENTS

1

The Time Traveler Returns

THE TIME TRAVELER (for so it will be convenient to speak of him) was expounding a recondite matter to us. His grey eyes shone and twinkled, and his usually pale face was flushed and animated. The fire burned brightly, and the soft radiance of the incandescent lights in the lilies of silver caught the bubbles that flashed and passed in our glasses. Our chairs, being his patents, embraced and caressed us rather than submitted to be sat upon, and there was that luxurious after-dinner atmosphere when thought runs gracefully free of the trammels of precision. It was Thursday again, and he put it to us in his usual way—marking the points with a lean forefinger—as we sat and lazily admired his earnestness over this latest paradox (as we thought it) and his fecundity.

"You must follow me carefully. I shall have to controvert one or two ideas that are almost universally accepted. The geometry, for instance, they taught you at school is founded on a misconception."

"Is not that rather a large thing to expect us to begin upon?" said Filby, an argumentative person with red hair.

"I do not mean to ask you to accept anything without reasonable ground for it. You will soon admit as much as I need from you. You know of course that a mathematical line, a line of thickness *nil*, has no real existence. They taught you that? Neither has a mathematical plane. These things are mere abstractions."

"That is all right," said the Psychologist.

"Nor, having only length, breadth, and thickness, can a cube have a real existence."

"There I object," said Filby. "Of course a solid body may exist. All real things—"

"So most people think. But wait a moment. Can an *instantaneous* cube exist?"

"Don't follow you," said Filby.

"Can a cube that does not last for any time at all, have a real existence?"

Filby became pensive.

"Clearly," the Time Traveler proceeded, "any real body must have extension in *four* directions: it must have length, breadth, thickness, and—duration. But through a natural infirmity of the flesh, which I will explain to you in a moment, we incline to overlook this fact. There are really four dimensions, three which we call the three planes of space, and a fourth, time. There is, however, a tendency to draw an unreal distinction between the former three dimensions and the latter, because it happens that our consciousness moves intermittently in one direction along the latter from the beginning to the end of our lives."

"That," said a very young man, making spasmodic efforts to relight his cigar over the lamp; "that ... very clear indeed."

"Now, it is very remarkable that this is so extensively overlooked," continued the Time Traveler, with a slight accession of cheerfulness. "Really this is what is meant by the fourth dimension, though some people who talk about the fourth dimension do not know they mean it. It is only another way of looking at time. *There is no difference between time and any of the three dimensions of space except that our consciousness moves along it.* But some foolish people have got hold of the wrong side of that idea. You have all heard what they have to say about this fourth dimension?"

"*I* have not," said the Provincial Mayor.

"It is simply this. That space, as our mathematicians have

it, is spoken of as having three dimensions, which one may call length, breadth, and thickness, and is always definable by reference to three planes, each at right angles to the others. But some philosophical people have been asking why *three* dimensions particularly—why not another direction at right angles to the other three?—and have even tried to construct a four-dimensional geometry. Professor Simon Newcomb was expounding this to the New York Mathematical Society only a month or so ago. You know how on a flat surface, which has only two dimensions, we can represent a figure of a three-dimensional solid, and similarly they think that by models of three dimensions they could represent one of four—if they could master the perspective of the thing. See?"

"I think so," murmured the Provincial Mayor; and, knitting his brows, he lapsed into an introspective state, his lips moving as one who repeats mystic words. "Yes, I think I see it now," he said after some time, brightening in a quite transitory manner.

"Well, I do not mind telling you I have been at work upon this geometry of four dimensions for some time. Some of my results are curious. For instance, here is a portrait of a man at eight years old, another at fifteen, another at seventeen, another at twenty-three, and so on. All these are evidently sections, as it were, three-dimensional representations of his four-dimensioned being, which is a fixed and unalterable thing.

"Scientific people," proceeded the Time Traveler, after the pause required for the proper assimilation of this, "know very well that time is only a kind of space. Here is a popular scientific diagram, a weather record. This line I trace with my finger shows the movement of the barometer. Yesterday it was so high, at night it fell, then this morning it rose again, and so gently upward to here. Surely the mercury did not trace this line in any of the dimensions of space generally recognized? But it traced such a line, and that line, therefore, we must conclude was along the time-dimension."

"But," said the Medical Man, staring hard at a coal in the fire, "if time is really only a fourth dimension of space, why is it, and why has it always been, regarded as something different? And why cannot we move in time as we move about in the other dimensions of space?"

The Time Traveler smiled. "Are you sure we can move freely in space? Right and left we can go, backward and forward freely enough, and men always have done so. I admit we move freely in two dimensions. But how about up and down? Gravitation limits us there."

"Not exactly," said the Medical Man. "There are balloons."

"But before the balloons, save for spasmodic jumping and the inequalities of the surface, man had no freedom of vertical movement."

"Still they could move a little up and down."

"Easier, far easier *down* than up."

"And you cannot move at all in time, you cannot get away from the present moment."

"My dear sir, that is just where you are wrong. That is just where the whole world has gone wrong. We are always getting away from the present moment. Our mental existences, which are immaterial and have no dimensions, are passing along the time-dimension with a uniform velocity from the cradle to the grave. Just as we should travel down if we began our existence fifty miles above the Earth's surface."

"But the great difficulty is this," interrupted the Psychologist. "You can move about in all directions of space, but you cannot move about in time."

"Why not?" said the Time Traveler.

"It's against reason," said Filby.

"What reason?" said the Time Traveler.

"You can show black is white by argument," said Filby, "but you will never convince me."

"Possibly not," said the Time Traveler. "But now you begin to see the object of my investigations into the geometry of four dimensions. Long ago I had a vague inkling of a machine—"

"To travel through time!" exclaimed the Very Young Man.

"That shall travel indifferently in any direction of space and time, as the driver determines."

Filby contented himself with laughter.

"But I have experimental verification," said the Time Traveler.

"It would be remarkably convenient for the historian," the Psychologist suggested. "One might travel back and verify the account of the Battle of Hastings, for instance!"

"Don't you think you would attract attention?" said the Medical Man. "Our ancestors had no great tolerance for anachronisms."

"One might get one's Greek from the very lips of Homer and Plato," the Very Young Man said.

"In which case they would certainly plough you for the Little Go. The German scholars have improved Greek so much."

"Then there is the future," said the Very Young Man. "Just think! One might invest all one's money, leave it to accumulate at interest, and hurry on ahead!"

"To discover a society," said I, "erected on a strictly communistic basis."

"Of all the wild extravagant theories!" began the Psychologist.

"Yes, so it seemed to me, but my aspirations are far greater still, so I never talked of it until—"

"Experimental verification!" cried I. "You are going to verify *that*?"

"The experiment!" cried Filby, who was getting brain-weary.

"Let's see your experiment anyhow," said the Psychologist, "though it's all humbug, you know."

The Time Traveler smiled round at us. Then, still smiling faintly, and with his hands deep in his trousers pockets, he walked slowly out of the room, and we heard his slippers shuffling down the long passage to his laboratory.

The Psychologist looked at us. "I wonder what he's got?"

"Some sleight-of-hand trick or other," said the Medical Man, and Filby tried to tell us about a conjurer he had seen at Burslem; but before he had finished his preface, the Time Traveler came back, and Filby's anecdote collapsed.

2

The Time Machine

THE THING THE TIME TRAVELER held in his hand was a glittering metallic framework, scarcely larger than a small clock, and very delicately made. There was ivory in it, and some transparent crystalline substance. He took one of the small octagonal tables that were scattered about the room, and then set it in front of the fire, with two legs on the hearthrug. On this table he placed the mechanism. Then he drew up a chair, and sat down. The only other object on the table was a small shaded lamp, the bright light of which fell full upon the model. There were also perhaps a dozen candles about, two in brass candlesticks upon the mantel and several in sconces, so that the room was brilliantly illuminated. I sat in a low arm-chair nearest the fire, and I drew this forward so as to be almost between the Time Traveler and the fireplace. Filby sat behind him, looking over his shoulder. The Medical Man and the Provincial Mayor watched him in profile from the right, the Psychologist from the left. The Very Young Man stood behind the Psychologist. We were all on the alert. It appears incredible to me that any kind of trick, however subtly conceived and however adroitly done, could have been played upon us under these conditions.

The Time Traveler looked at us, and then at the mechanism.

"Well?" said the Psychologist.

"This little affair," said the Time Traveler, resting his elbows upon the table and pressing his hands together above the apparatus, "is only a model. It is my plan for a machine to travel through time. You will notice that it looks singularly askew, and that there is an odd twinkling appearance about this bar, as though it was in some way unreal." He pointed to the part with his finger. "Also, here is one little white lever, and here is another."

The Medical Man got up out of his chair and peered into the thing. "It's beautifully made," he said.

"It took a great deal of time to make," retorted the Time Traveler. Then, when we had all imitated the action of the Medical Man, he said: "Now, I want you clearly to understand that this lever, being pressed over, sends the machine gliding into the future, and this other reverses the motion. This saddle represents the seat of a time traveler. Presently I am going to press the lever, and off the machine will go. It will vanish, pass into future time, and disappear. Have a good look at the thing. Look at the table, too, and satisfy yourselves there is no trickery. I don't want to waste this model, and then be told I'm a quack."

There was a minute's pause perhaps. The Psychologist seemed about to speak to me, but changed his mind. Then the Time Traveler put forth his finger towards the lever. "No," he said suddenly. "Lend me your hand." And turning to the Psychologist, he took that individual's hand in his own and told him to put out his forefinger.

We all saw the lever turn. I am absolutely certain there was no trickery. The engine started. There was a breath of wind, and the lamp flame jumped. One of the candles on the mantel was blown out, and the little machine began to tremble, then coughed and sputtered and was absolutely still.

Everyone was silent for a minute. Then Filby said he was damned. The Time Traveler ran a hand through his hair. "Well," he said, "perhaps after a few minor adjustments...."

The Psychologist slapped his hand against his leg in disappointment, and we stared at each other. "Look here," said the Medical Man, "are you in earnest about this? Or are you deliberately wasting our time?"

The Time Traveler stood up and moved to the tobacco jar on the mantel, and with his back to us began to fill his pipe. "A minor adjustment, that's all." He stooped to light a spill at the fire. Then he turned, lighting his pipe. "What is more, I have *another* machine nearly finished in there"—he indicated the laboratory—"and when that is put together, I mean to have a journey on my own account!"

The Psychologist began to shuffle his feet, and the Medical Man turned away, his face flushed with embarrassment.

"Here, let me show you the full-sized model," continued the Time Traveler. And thence, taking the lamp in his hand, he led the way down the long, drafty corridor to his laboratory. I remember vividly the flickering light, his queer, broad head in silhouette, the dance of the shadows, how we all followed him, puzzled but incredulous. In the laboratory we beheld stacks of books and papers piled high upon the stone floor, and broken glass everywhere. It looked as if we'd entered an alien formicary, as some of the mounds were nearly as tall as the Time Traveler himself. There was a workbench with phials of chemicals of various color; and against one wall was a blackboard covered with diagrams and formulae, while on another were pinned hand-written notes, as well as several blurry photographs of a young woman. (I recognized one of them as a picture taken with the Time Traveler during the last winter carnival, dated 1889.) In the center of the room was an antique arm-chair from which hundreds of electrical wires protruded, like snakes from the head of Medusa. Resting on its seat cushion were a bar and lever, presently uninstalled, that were similar in appearance to what we had seen on the prototype.

"Look here," said the Medical Man, "are you perfectly serious? Or is this all a trick—like that ghost you showed us last Christmas?"

"I was never more serious in my life," he exclaimed, holding the lamp aloft. "Through the application of science and mind—I am going to succeed. I intend to travel in time, and I will raise up this fallen world!"

None of us quite knew how to take it, and then I caught Filby's eye over the shoulder of the Medical Man. He winked at me solemnly.

3

The Time Traveler Returns

AT THAT TIME, I think, none of us quite believed in the Time Traveler. The fact is, the Time Traveler was one of those men who are often too clever to be believed: you never felt that you saw all round him; you always suspected some subtle reserve, some ingenuity in ambush, behind his lucid frankness. Had Filby shown the model and explained the matter in the Time Traveler's words, we should have shown *him* far less skepticism. For we should have perceived his motives: a pork butcher could understand Filby. But the Time Traveler had more than a touch of whim among his elements, and his motivations could seem simultaneously virtuous and ill-conceived, noble but also self-serving, and we distrusted him. Things that would have made the fame of a less clever man seemed tricks in his hands. It is a mistake to do things too easily. The serious people who took him seriously never felt quite sure of his deportment: they were somehow aware that trusting their reputations for judgment with him was like furnishing a nursery with egg-shell china. So I don't think any of us said very much about time traveling in the interval between that Thursday and the next, though its odd potentialities ran, no doubt, in most of our minds. Our hope fixed on its plausibility; our imagination, the curious paradoxes it suggested; and our desire, its restorative prospects. For my own part, though, I was preoccupied with the mania of our host. That I remember discussing with the Medical Man, whom I met outside the War Office a day after the failed experiment. He had just returned from a presentation by MacPherson and

Harrison describing the latest Tube Helmet, or "gas mask," designed to protect our soldiers from the noxious chemicals the Germans were using. Here were scientists, I thought, with an urgency—an obsessive mania—similar to our friend's.

The next Thursday I went again to Richmond—I suppose I was one of the Time Traveler's most constant guests—and, arriving late, found four or five men already assembled in his drawing-room. The Medical Man was standing before the fire with a sheet of paper in one hand. He glanced at his wristwatch. I looked round for the Time Traveler, and—"It's half-past seven now," said the Medical Man. He tapped the face of his Rolex. "I suppose we'd better have dinner?"

"Where's—?" said I, naming our host.

"You've just come? It's rather odd. He's 'unavoidably detained.' He asks me in this note to lead off with dinner at seven if he's not back. Says he'll explain when he comes."

"It seems a pity to let the dinner spoil," said the Editor of a well-known daily paper; and thereupon the Medical Man rang the bell. The Psychologist was the only person besides the Medical Man and myself who had attended the previous dinner. The other three men were the editor aforementioned, a certain journalist, and another—a quiet, shy man with a beard—whom I didn't know, and who, as far as my observation went, never opened his mouth all the evening. There was some speculation at the dining-table about our host's absence, and I suggested "time traveling," in a half-jocular spirit. The Editor wanted that explained to him, and the Psychologist volunteered an account of the "anticlimax" we had witnessed that day week. He was in the midst of his exposition when the door from the corridor opened slowly and without noise. I was facing the door, and saw it first. "Hallo!" I said. "At last!" And then the door opened wider, and the Time Traveler stood before us. I gave a cry of surprise.

"Good heavens, man! What's the matter?" cried the Medical Man, who saw him next. And the whole tableful turned towards the door.

He was in an amazing plight. His coat was dusty and dirty, and smeared with oil down the sleeves; his hair disordered, and as it seemed to me greyer—either with dust and dirt or because its color had actually faded. His face was ghastly pale; his chin had a brown cut on it—a cut half-healed; his expression was haggard and drawn, as by intense suffering. For a moment he hesitated in the doorway, as if he had been dazzled by the light. Then he came into the room. He walked with just such a limp as I have seen in footsore boys back from the Western Front. We stared at him in silence, expecting him to speak.

He said not a word, but came painfully to the table and made a motion towards the wine. The Editor filled a glass, and pushed it towards him. He drained it, and it seemed to do him good: for he looked round the table, and the ghost of his old smile flickered across his face.

"What on earth have you been up to, man?" said the Medical Man. The Time Traveler did not seem to hear.

"Don't let me disturb you," he said, with a certain faltering articulation. "I'm all right." He stopped, held out his glass for more, and took it off at a draft. "That's good," he said. His eyes grew brighter, and a faint color came into his cheeks. His glance flickered over our faces with a certain dull approval, and then went round the warm and comfortable room. Then he spoke again, still as if he were feeling his way among his words. "I'm going to wash, and then I'll come down and explain things…. Save me some of that mutton. I'm starving for a bit of meat."

He looked across at the Editor, who was a rare visitor. The Editor pushed back in his wheel-chair and began a question. "Tell you presently," said the Time Traveler. "I'm—funny! Be all right in a minute."

He put down his glass, and walked towards the staircase

door. Again I remarked his lameness and the soft padding sound of his footfall, and standing up in my place, I saw his feet as he went out. He had nothing on them but a pair of tattered blood-stained socks. Then the door closed upon him. I had half a mind to follow, 'til I remembered how he detested any fuss about himself. For a minute, perhaps, my mind was wool-gathering. Then, "Remarkable Behavior of an Eminent Scientist," I heard the Editor say, thinking (after his wont) in headlines. And this brought my attention back to the bright dining-table.

"What's the game?" said the Journalist. "Has he been doing the Amateur Cadger? I don't follow." I met the eye of the Psychologist, and read my own interpretation in his face. I thought of the Time Traveler limping painfully upstairs. I don't think anyone else had noticed his lameness.

The first to recover completely from this surprise was the Medical Man, who rang the bell—the Time Traveler hated to have servants waiting at dinner—for a hot plate. At that the Editor turned to his knife and fork with a grunt, and the Silent Man followed suit. The dinner was resumed. Conversation was exclamatory for a little while, with gaps of wonderment; and then the Editor got fervent in his curiosity. "Does our friend eke out his modest income as a sweeper? Or has he his Nebuchadnezzar phases?" he inquired.

"I feel assured it's this business of his fiancée, and of the time machine," I said, and took up the Psychologist's account of our previous meeting. The new guests were frankly incredulous. The Editor raised objections.

"What *was* this time traveling? A man couldn't cover himself with dust by rolling in a paradox, could he?" And then, as the idea came home to him, he resorted to caricature. Hadn't they any clothes-brushes in the future? The Journalist, too, would not believe at any price, and joined the Editor in the easy work of heaping ridicule on the whole thing. They were both the new kind of journalist— very joyous, irreverent young men. "Our Special

Correspondent in the Day after Tomorrow reports," the Journalist was saying—or rather shouting—when the Time Traveler came back. He was now dressed in ordinary evening clothes, and nothing save his haggard look remained of the change that had startled me.

"I say," said the Editor hilariously, "these chaps here say you have been learning how to travel into the middle of next week! Tell us all about Squiffy Asquith, will you? Munitions or suffragettes?"

The Time Traveler came to the place reserved for him without a word. He smiled quietly, in his old way. "Where's my mutton?" he said. "What a treat it is to stick a fork into meat again!"

"Story!" cried the Editor.

"Story be damned!" said the Time Traveler. "I want something to eat. I won't say a word until I get some peptone into my arteries. Thanks. And the salt."

"One word," said I. "Have you been time traveling?"

The Psychologist interrupted. "Of course he has! We all have. We are all traveling through time, inevitably forward."

"Yes, that's true," said the Time Traveler, with his mouth full, nodding his head.

The Time Traveler pushed his glass towards the Silent Man and rang it with his finger-nail; at which the Silent Man, who had been staring at his face, started convulsively, and poured him wine. The rest of the dinner was uncomfortable. For my own part, sudden questions kept on rising to my lips, and I dare say it was the same with the others. The Journalist tried to relieve the tension by telling anecdotes of "Mick" Mannock, flying ace. The Time Traveler, however, devoted his attention to his dinner, and displayed the appetite of a tramp. The Medical Man smoked a cigarette, and watched the Time Traveler through his eyelashes. The Silent Man drank gin with regularity and determination out of sheer nervousness. At last the Time Traveler pushed his plate away, and looked round us.

"I suppose I must apologize," he said. "I was simply starving. I've had a most amazing time." He reached out his hand for a cigar, and cut the end. "But come into the smoking-room. I have something to show you all, and it's better without greasy plates." And ringing the bell in passing, he led the way into the adjoining room.

"You have told the others about the time machine?" he said to me, leaning back in his easy-chair and naming the three new guests. The seven of us were now seated comfortably in a circle.

I nodded.

"Well," he said aloud, "I have made another."

4

The Half-time Machine

"LET ME START by saying that the concept of journeying from one time to another goes back nearly two thousand years. It is not a novelty. There is an ancient Sanskrit epic which describes the story of a king who travels briefly to Heaven, but when he returns to Earth, many years have passed. In the Theravada Buddhist tradition, there are explicit references to the fluid nature of the passage of time. In the *Payasi Sutta*, for example, one of the Buddha's disciples explains how time in the Heavens passes differently than it does on Earth."

There were several wary glances among tonight's guests. Finally, the Medical Man remarked, "That's all well and fine, but if this is to be another exposition on the theory of time travel, I can't see what this has to do with *science*. Myths are just that, and anyone can tell a ripping yarn."

Our host took a puff on his cigar. "I present these stories for two reasons. First, to make clear that there is a historic precedent for those concerned with journeying in time. If you were to think me mad, I do not want it so for that reason alone. I'm not sure I successfully dissuaded you on this front last week."

"That is certainly true," the Psychologist confirmed, and there was a bit of cautious laughter around the table.

"The second reason," our host continued, "is that in nearly all the ancient texts I have investigated, time travel is in the forward direction only, never backward. If you think about this, it is not surprising. As you yourself explained"—

he looked to the Psychologist—"we are *all* time travelers in that each of us is moving forward through time. We are born, we grow old, we die. Traveling into the future is not theoretical: it is, in fact, inexorable and axiomatic. So it is only natural we should start to think about it that way."

Our host took a leisurely drag on his cigar to give us time to assimilate this assumption. "Of course, going forward in time addresses only half the puzzle of time travel. We experience our lives as if pushed off a cliff: gravity is time, and we are forever falling into the future. We cannot fly by nature, nor can we control our descent, neither slower nor faster, or so it seems."

"It does indeed," said the Medical Man.

"And yet how quickly do we fall? What is the speed of life? How do we measure it? How do we know it never changes?"

The room fell silent as each of us pondered this latest paradox.

"Let me tell you the answer," the Time Traveler began. "There is no such thing as a singular speed of life. It is an illusion, a false assumption, and it is exactly where I erred last week. While we are all moving through time, tracing a geometric path in the fourth dimension just as we do in the other three—*we are not each one of us traveling at the same speed.*"

"Explain," the Editor demanded.

"Quite simply, the perception of time is relative to the observer."

"What?"

The Time Traveler took another leisurely drag on his cigar. "Perhaps you are familiar with this: 'When you sit with a good friend for two hours, you think it is only a minute; but when you sit on a hot stove for a minute, you think it is two hours.'"

The Medical Man's brow furrowed as if he were trying to recall the provenance of the aphorism. Finally, he spoke up.

"I think you've lost me. I acknowledge the mind may distort one's perception of time. In imagination or memory, certainly, we can speed up or slow down its passage. But I believe you must be suggesting more than that. Unless your latest breakthrough is to imagine or recollect your way to the past or future—to *pretend* to travel through time!"

"Of course not." The Time Traveler jabbed his cigar towards the Medical Man. "But it is critical you apprehend, at least intuitively, that one's current frame of reference affects the passage of time."

"Surely you can provide us with a better example," the Journalist said. "Something less fanciful."

"Very well. Imagine you are on a train. You look out the window and there is a second train beside yours, apparently motionless. You see a passenger on that train. He's looking out the window, too, and he waves. How fast is the other passenger moving?"

The Medical Man answered first: "He's not moving at all. You just said so. It's a silly question."

The Time Traveler picked up a small plate and then stubbed out his cigar. "From your point of view, yes, it seems obvious: the other passenger is not moving at all. His position, relative to yours, remains constant. Yet suppose both trains are moving on parallel tracks at the same speed. Wouldn't that other passenger appear to be still, even though he is unquestionably moving?"

The Medical Man thought for a moment and then nodded. "Yes. I suppose that's true. Relative to me, and modulo any revealing vibration, the other passenger wouldn't appear to be moving at all, even if he were in fact."

"Now imagine both trains are passing through a station. If someone were standing on the platform as the trains passed, and if this person saw you through the window, would they think you were moving or not?"

The Medical Man sat upright. "Moving. Definitely moving."

"Good. And now I'll have you imagine one last circumstance. Imagine there's another train. It's on your track, heading straight towards you."

"I'm not sure I like this scenario," the Editor said.

"From the point of view of the man on the platform, both your train and this new train appear to be moving towards each other at the same speed. But if you were to lean out the window of your coach, how fast would you say this new train was approaching?"

The Medical Man paused to think. "Now *that* is an interesting question."

The Editor jumped in. "Twice as fast! Because from our point of view, the speed of the oncoming train is influenced by the speed of our own, racing towards it."

The Medical Man nodded. "Ah, yes, of course. That does make sense."

The Time Traveler stood and stretched, and then walked to the sidebar where he opened a bottle of Cognac. He filled six snifters and passed them around the circle, first to the Medical Man on his right and then to the Journalist on his left. "Now I must apologize. I said that I wanted you to apprehend, at least intuitively, how one's current frame of reference might affect the perception of space and time. This I have accomplished. Unfortunately, what I am going to tell you now is something which is nearly impossible to intuit, but is true nonetheless. Have you heard of the theory of special relativity."

The Journalist nodded first, and a few other guests imitated him. "It's Einstein," he said. "That German fellow. He describes how nothing can travel faster than the speed of light, and some uncanny consequences that result. I'm guessing that's what you want to tackle next."

"Yes, exactly. Einstein explained how two observers moving at constant velocity relative to one another may measure the passage of time differently."

The Medical Man interrupted: "Hold on, you said if our

two passengers in the coach were moving at the same speed, it would appear to each that they weren't moving at all. Surely time passes the same for each of them?"

"That's where Einstein's work becomes so interesting. Let's return to the train station for a moment. Imagine that the man on the platform has a cricket ball, and that he hurls it down the track at a speed of one hundred miles per hour."

"A decent delivery," the Journalist said.

"Imagine if instead he is on the moving train, and he bowls straight down the aisle. How fast would *that* ball be going?"

"Let me try," the Medical Man said. "I think I'm getting the hang of this. From the point of view of the bowler, the ball would still be flying a hundred miles per hour, but from the point of view of someone observing him as the train passed the platform, the ball would be appear to be traveling faster. In fact, it would be one hundred miles per hour added to the speed of the train."

"Correct. Now let's modify our scenario. Suppose the man on the platform has an electric torch instead of a cricket ball, and he shines the torch down the track. The light from the torch will fly down the track at a speed of 186,000 miles per second—"

"It's remarkable," interrupted the Journalist, "that we were ever able to determine the speed of something as intangible as light."

"It is an interesting story," our host answered, "how the Danish astronomer Olaus Roemer first made his measurements; but it is irrelevant to today's discussion."

"Yes, yes," the Journalist said. "Forgive the intrusion."

"To continue: imagine our man with the torch is not on the platform, but instead on the moving train, and he shines the torch down the aisle. How fast would the light appear to be moving relative to our various observers?"

The Medical Man shook his head: "I fear this is a trick question, so I'll let you answer it for us."

Our host looked round the circle of his guests. "Very well. This is where it gets rather non-intuitive, because according to Einstein the light from the torch would appear to travel at the *same speed* for *all our observers*."

"How is that possible!" the Editor declared.

"The science is complicated, so I won't bore you with details. But I can describe the consequence of the fact, because it has a direct implication for my new prototype."

"So you have another invention!" I exclaimed. "I was wondering if we were to get back to that!"

The Time Traveler nodded and then returned to his final scenario. "Imagine two people," he said. "A woman in a space-ship traveling to a planet 9.5 light-years from Earth at 95 percent of the speed of light, and her daughter who remains on Earth. For the daughter, tracking her mother through a telescope on Earth, the trip appears to take ten years."

"Makes perfect sense," the Medical Man exclaimed. "The numbers work out."

"For the woman on the space-ship, however, as a consequence of Einstein's theory of special relativity, she experiences a trip of much shorter duration. For her, the trip takes only three years, and were she to turn round and return to Earth, a total of six years would have passed for her."

"It seems absurd," the Medical Man said.

"Unintuitive, perhaps, but not absurd. The maths bears this out. And remember, when the woman arrives back on Earth, *twenty years* will have gone by for her daughter. Our spacefarer would have effectively traveled into the future!"

"Remarkable!" said I.

"Of course we don't have space-ships that travel at such relativistic speeds, at least not yet."

"I should say not!" the Journalist exclaimed. "Or I would be writing about that every week."

The Medical Man waved a hand at the Journalist. "Let our host continue."

"It is true we do not yet have space-faring vessels that can travel at such astounding speeds; however, the relativistic effects can be replicated without traveling to the stars, and I have done so!"

The Medical Man raised an eyebrow. The rest of the circle remained silent, then at last the Editor spoke. "Surely, the proof of the pudding is in the tasting," he said.

The Journalist followed on: "You said you'd made another mechanism. If this is not a trick, show us."

The Time Traveler finished the last of his brandy, and then stood. He held up his forefinger for us to wait, and then departed the room, returning a moment later with a wooden box about the size of an electric toaster. He placed it on a small table near the door and carefully unpacked its contents as we all gathered round. This second prototype was clearly a modification of the first, although this one had a collection of tiny prisms and mirrors arranged in sequence surrounding the central leather saddle. The mechanism looked rather like an imperial crown with arches and a band, although at the apex, rather than a cross, were several tiny levers capped with jewels—a sapphire, an emerald, a ruby. The overall design had an aesthetic that was both beautiful and a little terrifying.

"This device uses a rotating cylinder of light to twist space-time, and anything within the ring is similarly twisted—much the way cream moves round the top of your coffee after you swirl it with a spoon. The result is that both the device and its driver move at relativistic speed. I have modified this prototype to travel a mere decade into the future, although I have calculated that one might travel as fast as six hundred years an hour!"

Our host's excitement was palpable, and it was impossible in that moment not to feel the legitimacy and triumph of this latest invention. We all leaned over the table to get as close a look at the device as possible. Like the majestic crown it resembled, it conveyed a kind of glory. I said as much.

"Glory? Yes, yes, that's good. Perhaps immortality and resurrection, too. Of course this is simply a first step. This affair can travel into the future only, and I must move both forward and backward to complete my real work."

The Psychologist threw me a worried glance, but before he could say anything, the Time Traveler put forth his finger towards the sapphire lever. We all saw the lever roll forward, and a golden beam of light began to race round the crown, each mirror catching the light of the previous one and passing it on to the next, each prism splitting the beam, again and again, round and round, and amplifying in luminosity. We drew back at the sudden warmth emanating from the mechanism, then shielded our eyes as the light grew painfully bright. A shrill whine came next, like a fingernail on a blackboard, and we switched to covering our ears.

Almost immediately the saddle ignited in a burst of flame, followed by the most terrible stench of burning metal as one of the arches began to melt. Grey smoke billowed from the device, covering everything, and then the machine itself went dark, throwing the room into a temporal night. It took a moment for my eyes to adjust, and when they did I saw Mrs. Watchett throwing a small blanket over the smoldering remains of the mechanism.

"Dear me!" she exclaimed. "Dear me! Dear me!" And without hesitation the Journalist and the Medical Man grabbed glass and pitcher from another table and doused the blanket with water. The room was an absolute mess, the air was thick with acrid smoke, and I could see a dark stain on the ceiling above the covered device.

Our host stood back from the conflagration, his eyes wide, a smear of ash across his cheek. He shook his head, exhaled, and then folded his arms. "I may have made a slight miscalculation."

5

The Time Traveler Returns

THE NEXT THURSDAY, I was the first to arrive for dinner. If there were additional effects upon the house as a result of last week's fire, I could not say. For as Hillyer showed me down the hallway and into the drawing-room, I was distracted by a viper's nest of cables of various color and thickness running along the floor. Once in the drawing-room, it was even worse: generators, miniature dynamos, and power coils covered most of the carpet, along with at least half-a-dozen flexible aluminum ducts—some as large as two feet in circumference—snaking every which way. One duct, perhaps a foot in diameter, came in the door from the dining-room, then disappeared out the door to the staircase. Another disappeared into a hole cut into the ceiling.

The Medical Man arrived next. "What's all this!" he shouted, and only then did I realize the chaos of the house extended into the auditory realm. Every engine was idling, and it was as if we had stepped onto a factory floor. Together we followed one of the ducts into the dining-room, where we found cables running along the walls like African vines, even depending from the chandelier. Two large fans were spinning at opposite ends of the room and a petrol generator was pushed up against the sideboard. It was not only noisy here, but smelly, too. The dining-table in the center of the room was clear of the mechanical confusion, at least, and impeccably set, though I wondered how Mrs. Watchett might possibly navigate the dining-room to serve us all our supper.

The Journalist arrived next, and a man I didn't know who was introduced to me as an auxiliary bishop from the diocese of Bath and Wells in the province of Canterbury. We shook hands and exchanged pleasantries, as best we could. When the Silent Man arrived, he looked round at the clutter of wires and ducts, his mouth agape.

"Well," said the Medical Man, "The table is set for six and there are five of us now. I suppose our host is to be late again. Perhaps we should all be seated."

As we arranged ourselves around the table, the Time Traveler surprised us by bursting through the door from the passage that led to his laboratory. He was dressed in his work clothes—a dirty canvas apron over wool trousers and colorless shirt—and he nearly tripped over a twisted loop of cable as he stumbled into the room.

"I say!" exclaimed the Bishop. "Are you all right?"

I stood and joined the Bishop in extending a hand to our host. He looked much the same as the week last—disheveled and distraught. The Bishop was clearly surprised by his appearance, having not seen him before; still, when I noticed the slash of soot on our host's cheek, unwashed since our last encounter, my concern increased.

"I'm fine, I'm fine," he mumbled, and shoo'd us away. For a moment he regarded us as strangers, I think, but the confusion passed quickly. "It's Thursday again, isn't it," he said, and I was relieved it was more statement than question. His eyes immediately brightened and he made his way round the table shaking each of our hands. He rang the bell for dinner, although I was skeptical his housekeepers would hear it over the cacophony of the generator and fans.

"Perfect timing," he declared. "I have just completed my latest prototype. And it is *fully* functional—past and future. I've done it! I've done it!" He clapped the Medical Man on his back.

There followed a number of questions from around the table; however, once the Time Traveler sat, he steered the conversation away from the most essential topics. He talked instead about the weather, the cricket. We even dallied in politics when the Bishop made several surprisingly uncharitable remarks about Unity Mitford. It seemed the denial by our host of both his mania and his grief was complete. By the time dessert was served, however, the Journalist could no longer contain himself.

"These cables!" he said. "And ducts! My dear sir, are we not going to discuss what you have done to your home?" He waved his hand wildly in the air. "Your house has become—some sort of living organism! And with hardly any room for the human."

The Time Traveler burst out laughing. "Terribly sorry! I've been so focused all week. I need a moment ... to clear my head. Of course this all must be quite the shock."

"It is astounding," the Medical Man agreed, and I could hear the worry in his voice.

Our host cleared a space, pushing his teacup and dessert plate to the side. In their place, he pulled from his pocket a small flat disk and placed it on the table.

"This is it. This is my latest invention."

The table fell silent, and there was some trepidation as we all leaned in for a closer look. The disk was white and smooth as marble, and about the size of a penny. If this really was his latest invention, it was a total revamp of his original design. The Time Traveler spread his fingers and brushed his hands over the tablecloth, smoothing back any wrinkles around the disk. The act suggested care and attention, but also a kind of veneration. His eyes remained on his latest invention as he began the evening's discourse.

"I must first confess," he said. "My exploration of geometry without taking into account the effect of relativity was an oversight. And then last week, I made two additional errors. The first was attempting to solve the problem of time travel by simplifying it—or rather, *over*-simplifying it. That is, considering travel along a single axis, the fourth dimension, in a single direction—forward. It's like trying to solve the problem of tying your shoe by using only the right-hand lace. As the great man said, everything should be made as simple as possible, but no simpler."

"That's Einstein, again," said the Medical Man.

Our host nodded. "Yes. And it was also thanks to Einstein that I realized my second mistake—studying macro-scale motion without appreciating micro-scale quantum mechanics. Simple relativistic physics, classical chemistry, and basic geometry describe the universe above the level of sub-atomic particles. However, a deeper understanding of general relativity and quantum physics is necessary to describe very small particles, and a mastery of both levels, the quantum and the relativistic, is necessary to untangle the Gordian knot of time travel."

The Journalist put down his cup. "I am afraid this is all getting beyond me. I understand geometry—every schoolboy suffers the academic persuasion of Pythagoras and Euclid. But relativistic physics? Sub-atomic particles? I just don't know." The Journalist was speaking for all of us, as a tableful of heads nodded up and down, but such was the charismatic nature of our host that we were also intrigued.

"I will break it down. There are just three things to understand. First, there are four dimensions, three in space, one in time. I think you are by now all familiar with this."

We all agreed. "Length, breadth, thickness, and duration," said I.

"Second, you must understand that individuals move through these dimensions in various directions and at various speeds, and that their motions are relative to one another. It was considering just this aspect of relativity that I designed last week's prototype."

The Bishop raised his hand. "I am sure you have explained this before, but I'm wondering if you might dwell on this second point a little longer."

The Medical Man came to his assistance: "Think of it this way, Bishop…," he began, offering as example the metaphor of trains, passengers, and cricket balls—what we had all discussed that Thursday week.

The Bishop nodded enthusiastically. "Yes, I can see that now. How fascinating that I had never once before considered this!"

The Time Traveler continued: "Third," he said, "you must understand that these four dimensions are not independent. What affects one dimension may affect the others. By analogy"—he turned to the Bishop—"imagine a well-made bed, with a tight sheet. The sheet has length and breadth, but it also has thickness and duration. If I place a cannon ball in the center of the bed, it will sink, stretching the sheet. That is to say, deforming its length and breadth— but it will deform all of its dimensions, in fact."

The Bishop clapped his hands together. "Remarkable! Everything you say sounds quite preposterous at first, and yet after a few supplementary words you have run circles around my doubt!" (I wondered idly if the Bishop's congregation had a similar experience with his interpretation of chapter and verse, but before I could raise the question, the Time Traveler concluded his argument.)

"Now, it is by combining all three of these premises— geometry, macro-scale general relativity, and micro-scale quantum field theory—that I can govern motion through time and space in a manner that is both reversible and wholly self-consistent at any scale!"

"I fear you may have lost us again," said the Journalist.

"Perhaps then it is better to demonstrate."

6

The Multi-megawatt Machine

OUR HOST ASKED US not to touch the flat disk he had placed on the table. He then disappeared down the passage to his laboratory and returned moments later, carrying a steel junction box under one arm and dragging a long cable after him.

"I've removed this power line from my full-sized mock-up, but it will work just as well with this smaller prototype. You may want to step back."

He placed the junction box on the table, and then wired in the cable he had brought from his laboratory. Once he had finished, he added a line from the petrol generator, as well as two of the electrical lines hanging from the chandelier. The dining-room lights began to flicker.

"I am drawing energy from several megawatt electrical stations, including Kingston, Battersea A, and Acton Lane, as well as from my own generators. Matter and radiation manifest as a capacity to perform work, and my invention has an insatiable appetite for power. There may be some sparks."

There were no sparks, but several questions. "How do you side-step the petrol rations?" the Journalist asked. "Is there a special green book for inventors?"

The Psychologist raised his hand. "I was wondering that myself. How does this affect the war effort?"

"Is there a military application?" the Medical Man asked. "Something to knock back Hitler?"

The Time Traveler ignored these queries and continued

to prepare his prototype. The output line from the junction box was tripartite, and each wire ended in a tiny bead of copper. He touched these to the white disk, and they connected with a magnetic click. The petrol generator gave a sudden whoosh as the throttle opened, and from round the house I could hear several more engines roar to life.

Rather than heed our host's warning, most of us leaned in closer to get a better look at the operation of this unlikely and utterly alien contraption. At first, nothing happened. The disk remained inanimate, although the dining-room lights continued to flicker. Then I heard a kind of rumble, like the sound of distant waves crashing against a shore. Whether it emanated from one of the disk's many power sources or from the disk itself, I couldn't say. But even in the flickering light we could see that the center of the white disk had darkened, and this dark stain seemed to be spreading.

"The full-sized model has two interior seats, for I hope to offer one of you the opportunity to accompany me on my first voyage through time. This prototype, however, is independent. That is, it is not designed to carry anything."

By this time the dark stain had overcome the disk. It was now entirely black—obsidian, in fact—but the Medical Man was the first to identify another change.

"It's like a balloon," he said, and indeed he had noticed something I had not. For not only had the disk darkened, but it had also started to inflate.

Our host grinned. "The principle is to trigger a localized distortion of space-time by generating a gravity well. This is why it requires so much energy. As the prototype grows heavier, doubling its mass every few seconds, you may feel light in the feet, or even a little light-headed. I estimate it's nearly five kilograms—ten pounds—already."

"It's a *perfect sphere*," said the Bishop, and I could hear both wonder and awe in his voice. The mechanism was now the size and shape of a clairvoyant's crystal ball.

"Indeed—and angels might have such purpose! I call this *ad extremum spatium* as the mechanism moves from two-dimensional disk to three-dimensional sphere. Watch as *ad consummationem saeculi* follows, when it begins to spread the lips of earthly matter, to press into the fourth dimension, shape-shifting, swelling, filling the virtual space of time. Soon the entire mechanism will approach the approximate mass of Jupiter—"

"Hold on!" the Journalist said, leveling his dessert spoon at the still-expanding sphere. "Are you suggesting that that—that black *thing*—will expand until it's the size of Jupiter!"

The table creaked and the Medical Man and the Silent Man both rose from their chairs. The sphere was now the size of a football, but it was no longer black, not exactly. It was so dismal in color, so negative, so unreal, that it looked more like it wasn't there at all—as if it were a hole in the fabric of the room. The table groaned under the increasing weight of the mechanism.

"Of course not," said the Time Traveler. "Don't be ridiculous. I told you the distortion is *localized*. The majority of its mass will be squeezed into the fourth dimension, and the weight of the prototype should increase to no more than five or six hundred kilograms. And dash it all, it's an Eastlake table! Walnut and rosewood. It will hold."

The Medical Man gasped: "*Six hundred kilograms!*"

The Time Traveler ignored him. "Once it reaches full mass—about the size of a beach ball, I think—it will distort space-time in exactly the manner I have specified, and the sphere will roll—literally roll—sixty-two years into the past."

"My God!" exclaimed the Bishop. "And where will it land?"

At this point, the house grew significantly louder. The generators and power coils were surely running hot, fans had accelerated in compensation, air and fluid swooshed noisily through the ducts, and sparks—spraying from cables that climbed the walls—sizzled as they touched the ground. Under my feet the floor began to shake. The Journalist had called the house a living organism—and that is exactly what it seemed. Some enormous beast, suffering under back-breaking exertion. The table creaked again, ominously this time, and I felt certain it would buckle. The time machine—the sphere, the black hole, *the beast*—was now at least a meter across. I started to back away from the table just as a black cloud rolled into the dining-room from the corridor that led to the laboratory. I was immediately overcome by its sudden stench of sulphur, and through its gloom I could see orange flashes of flame. Something was on fire.

"Here it goes!" cried our host. "Get ready! You may experience a slight change in pressure. *Ad finem omnia!* Eureka! Eureka!"

It was at that moment I heard the walnut and rosewood table collapse under the weight of the invention, as well a horrific explosion which knocked me off my feet; but I did not *see* any of it. There was a terrible flash of light first and then we were all at that moment plunged into the most abyssal darkness.

7

The Time Traveler Returns

I VISITED THE HOUSE several times the next week. The roof of the summer extension had partially collapsed, and fire had breached many of the main building's interior walls. There was a hole about three feet wide in the center of the dining-room where the six-hundred-kilogram black ball had plunged through the floor before turning inert, and many of the surrounding floorboards had been damaged. Much of the ground floor was still flooded with water and petrol, and everything stank of rot and brimstone. No one had been harmed in the accident, but everyone was shaken.

I saw the Time Traveler only on my second visit, but he was preoccupied with the reparations, and we spoke only briefly. I do remember his telling me he'd "miscalculated," and therewith followed a brief discourse on the nature of sub-atomic matter that I did not understand at all. He seemed as manic as he had been on the day of the accident.

A month passed before a group of us was summoned again—the Medical Man, Filby, the Journalist, the Psychologist, and myself—and we all decided to meet beforehand at the Lone Wolf, a pub a quarter mile from our friend's home in Richmond, across the river in Brentford. We discussed his "various electrical misadventures," as the Journalist put it, as well as what the Psychologist called (perhaps too colorfully) "a brave day sunk in hideous night." (In his defense, this was not long after the Great Smog.) The Medical Man suggested our friend might be suffering from a kind of dyschronometria, a distorted sense of time.

When we finally arrived at the house in Richmond, we were welcomed by a frail-seeming woman none of us had met previously. She introduced herself simply as our host's domestic and bid us call her Uhra. She was younger than Mrs. Watchett and smaller in stature, but pleasant and accommodating as she led us through the house. I admit I was not surprised to learn later that Mrs. Watchett had decided to leave our host's employ after the "miscalculation" of the previous month. I was, however, surprised by the refurbished state of our friend's residence. The drawing-room and smoking-room appeared as if they had never been damaged, and when Uhra switched on the lights in the dining-room, we were all taken aback by its renewed splendor. Hardwood covered the floor along with a dark green Wilton weave carpet, exactly as it had been before. The wallpaper was new—William Morris this time, an acanthus pattern, similar to that which covered the walls at St. James's Palace. Perhaps most unexpected of all, however, was the table in the middle of the room. Another bespoke Eastlake affair, walnut and rosewood, perfectly identical to the original design. I don't think I could begin to calculate the cost of such exquisite—and rapid—repairs and replacements.

"I say," said Filby. "This is not what I'd imagined after your description of his previous demonstration."

"Surprising, indeed," was all the Journalist had in reply.

The dining-table was set with linen and crystal—as it had been the last time we'd entertained a disquisition from the Time Traveler; and as before, a white vase with several small white flowers served as a centerpiece. There was one new addition to the table: a handmade hoop, approximately the size of a woman's bracelet. It was bamboo, or perhaps willow, strung with an uneven—or rather asymmetric—weave of silk or wool, so it could not be placed on a wrist. A single feather and cerulean bead were caught in its tiny web; and the entire thing was hanging from a small wooden stand, much like a tiny gong might suspend from its frame.

Our host (after his wont) was not yet in attendance; and the Medical Man (after *his* wont) suggested we might as well ring the bell and dine until such time as the Time Traveler returned. With no objections, he called for dinner and sat, and we followed suit. All of us noticed, I am sure, that the chairs around the dining-table, though similar to their previous design, were not exactly the same. As before they embraced and caressed us rather than submitted to be sat upon, but new knobs allowed one to adjust the pan, tilt, and roll of the seat. I am certain I have never sat in such a comfortable chair before or since; and were the inventor to license these new patents, I am certain another fortune would come his way. These were chairs so comfortable one might readily fall asleep in them!

Hillyer—whom I was pleased to discover was still in the employ of our host—came by with dessert, a fabulous three-layered Black Forest cake, after we'd finished our mains. He tuned the wireless to the BBC, the Third Programme, and Bach's *Brandenburg Concerto No. 3* filled the air as he informed us, first, that there would be no coffee this evening, and, second, that our host would arrive presently. True to Hillyer's word, the Time Traveler came downstairs ten minutes later. He looked rested and clean, bright and freshly showered. His grey eyes shone and twinkled, and he was fitter than I'd seen in many weeks. Only his attire gave us pause—he'd arrived in bedroom slippers, and wearing a long dark dress that I assumed was his nightgown. I tried not to stare.

"I regret not dining with you this evening," he said, "but routine necessitated an earlier meal. I suppose we will have to suffice with a companionable drink." He lifted a glass from the table and filled it to the brim with the Merlot. We joined him in a somewhat guarded toast.

"I'm just back from a short jog, you see, from the cemetery to Chiswick and back."

"The cemetery? Fulham Cemetery?"

"Yes, exactly, then to Chiswick near Turnham Green and back."

"Is that your nightshirt?" sputtered the Medical Man.

"Jogging!" Filby exclaimed, cutting in before our host could respond to the Medical Man's indelicate inquiry. "I can't believe it! And after that dreadful pea-souper!"

"I started a regimen last month—after our dinner. At first to clear my head, you understand. There was quite a lot of tidying-up to do."

The Psychologist looked as if he were about to speak, but our host began a long and involved re-accounting of the demolition and subsequent restoration of his home. He seemed overall pleased with the work and hardly seemed to take a breath as he recounted the many details and decisions, trivial and otherwise, necessary to make his home habitable again. Finally he paused in his discourse, and the Psychologist quickly put aside the bite of cake that was nearly to his mouth. He then pronounced what was on all our minds, but which no one had thus far dared to speak.

"All of this work is quite marvelous," he started, "and I am pleased to see you're attending to your health."

"I'm as healthy as I have ever been—healthier, in fact!"

"Yes, well, given what you've been through, and the complications with your inventions in the past—"

"Complications? A few setbacks, perhaps."

"Yes, of course, but—but I am obligated to ask: Have you finally discontinued your researches?"

The Time Traveler looked confused. "Researches?"

"Into time travel, blast it!" exclaimed Filby.

The Time Traveler broke out in laughter, and I am certain none of us knew quite how to interpret this response. He finished his Merlot off at a draft and returned the glass to the table. "I said I began my jogging regimen to clear my head, *at first*."

8

The Bedtime Machine

THE TIME TRAVELER paced the room as he began the evening's oration. "Are any of you familiar with the Jewish tradition? No?" He shook his head in disappointment. "I should have invited the Bishop this week, or a rabbi." He turned his head towards the door. *"Hillyer!"* he called, and a moment later his manservant appeared. "Let's find a rabbi. Can you do that?"

Hillyer bowed and exited, and our host, thus satisfied, resumed his pacing and his lecture.

"I've returned to the classics, you see. Not the physicists, certainly. They know a great deal but not enough, that is clear. So many mathematicians are anti-realist. Anything goes if it's internally consistent. But whether it has a bearing on reality? That's another matter entirely. So I've moved away from the mind, the little grey cells. I'm looking into the heart. It's something I should have done from the start. Time travel isn't a hard problem—it's a *heart* problem. It's been a heart problem from the very beginning."

We all glanced round the table. I suspect everyone was thinking the same thing. Had our host finally gone mad? He seemed physically healthy, certainly, and the idea of attaining a balance of heart and mind—well, that would be something. God knows he deserved it. But his dress—and his speech—marked him at least as disturbed as the month before.

"In the first century BCE, in the Jewish tradition," the Time Traveler explained, "a scholar named Honi ha-M'agel returned home one day to find his family and friends had all disappeared. No one recognized him, nor had heard of any of his friends. How could that be so?" He looked round the room. "Why, he had fallen asleep *for seventy years!* A familiar story, is it not? A common man who sleeps for years and awakens in a changed society. Surely some of you have heard similar tales?"

There was silence around the table. I think we were all still sizing up the present situation. Finally, the Journalist spoke. "There's *Looking Backward* by Edward Bellamy."

"Very good! Any others?"

I raised my glass. "I know another. In Charles Dickens' *A Christmas Carol*, Scrooge is transported in a kind of dream forward and backward in time."

Filby joined the game: "Very well, I know one, too. In *A Connecticut Yankee in King Arthur's Court,* an engineer in America is knocked on the head and is transported in time and space to the reign of King Arthur."

"All excellent examples! There is also 'Rip Van Winkle' by Washington Irving; *L'An 2440* by Louis-Sébastien Mercier; even *When the Sleeper Wakes* by our friend H.G. Wells. The Aranda people of Central Australia would call these examples of the Dreamtime, a spiritual and secret province that is every-where and every-when, a weave of the world, a space out of time."

At this point, our host focused on the Medical Man. "I can tell by your expression you think this is mad, and that I am suddenly anti-science."

"Honestly, I don't know what to think," the Medical Man opined.

"I understand your doubt. After all, you were the one who once questioned the value of myths, and worried that I fancied the key to time travel was in make-believe. But I am not talking about *pretending*, not at all!"

"But you've already tried thrice—and failed. Time travel is impossible. You simply cannot move round in time."

"You are wrong to say that we cannot move about in time. For instance, if I am recalling an incident very vividly, I go back to the instant of its occurrence: I become absent-minded, as you say. I jump back for a moment."

"That hardly counts!"

"Of course you may say we have no means of staying back for any length of time, any more than a four-legged beast has of staying six feet above the ground in our three dimensions. But a rational man is better off than the beast in this respect. As you yourself have said, he can go up against gravitation in a balloon or an airplane, and why should he not hope that ultimately he may be able to stop or accelerate his drift along the time-dimension, or even turn about and travel the other way?"

"Oh, this," began Filby, "is all—"

"It's not that I think the study of the arts takes precedence to that of the sciences; but that I am now taking them *both* into account. Art is a lie, yes, but a lie that lets us see the truth. If anything my vision is more clear than it has ever been. I know now how to travel in time. I will use imagination—powered by science and framed by the heart. I will undo the past. I will correct history. For it is in prolonged sleep, in *dreaming*, that I've found the key to time travel!"

The Medical Man slowly shook his head. "My friend, I do not think you mad. But this has been a difficult month for you." He looked round the table. "A difficult *year*," he added, and I daresay we all concurred.

For a moment the Time Traveler appeared disarmed, then discomfited. He suddenly clenched both hands into fists.

"Now you are all wasting my time! You are not listening. You think me not only a fool, but also an ignoramus. Do any of *you* understand the protocols of activation synthesis during sleep? Or the latest science behind defensive immobilization? Do you understand the mechanism of semantic imprinting that occurs while we dream? Of course not!—because you only criticize what you have not taken the time to understand. Have you heard of lucid dreaming, in which a dreamer is conscious of the fact that he is dreaming? Or of the Oneironauts of Skepsis? Like them, I have harnessed the broad warrant of dreaming and intend to use that authority!"

"How can you harness a dream?" Filby asked.

"That is the correct question—how! I will show you."

The Time Traveler then rang the bell. Uhra entered presently and cleared the dining-table, leaving only our glasses, the wine, and the strange bracelet I'd noticed earlier. When she left, the Journalist asked if our host had created another prototype, a mechanism to harness dreams and to voyage through time.

"I have," he acknowledged, "and it has been in front of you all evening." He pointed to the small hoop on the table. "In certain Native American cultures, the *asabikeshiinh*, as it is called, was designed as a kind of apotropaic charm. It is named after the inanimate form of the word for 'spider,' and you may have heard them called dream-catchers. I won't bore you with details, but each night for the past two weeks I have employed this *asabikeshiinh* to capture my dreams. And not just any dreams. I have loosed nightmares, absent-minded transgressions, and mere fancies, and saved only those dreams that occur on a specific date. Together the dreams reinforce themselves, in synergy."

"How do you dream of a specific date?" the Psychologist inquired.

The Journalist exclaimed, "Indeed! Tell us! I have been trying my entire life to pick what fancy fills my night's imaginings, preferably with stockings and a frou-frou, but to no avail!" The others laughed, but the Time Traveler ignored them.

"Like so many things in life, dream control improves with practice. It is quite simple, really."

For an instant I caught the eye of our host, and I knew he was dissembling, or at least stretching the truth. He may have developed some mastery over the time and place of his dreams, but I suspected in truth his dreams had mastery over him. I knew his sleep had been disturbed for some months now, and that he'd suffered from a frequent nightmare. *One time* and *one place* that he'd return to again and again, and with little control over the recurrence. None of the other guests seemed to catch this, however, and now Filby was raising his glass.

"And I suppose you plan a demonstration of this most minimal mechanism," Filby said, gesturing towards the dream-catcher.

"Exactly. A demonstration. Of course this is a mere prototype. Its ability to travel back in time is circumscribed by the number of dreams it may store. The full-sized model will have no limitation. We will be able to travel hundreds of years."

"We?"

"Oh, yes! If you so choose, you may all join me." He bowed slightly. "You are invited."

The Medical Man finished his wine, put his glass down, and seemed about to speak. But he must have thought better of it, and instead picked up his glass again and rolled it pensively between his fingers.

"I have had my evening's exercise," the Time Traveler said. "That's why I was jogging. I am well-fed, and I've had my drink. I have emptied my bladder, too. All of these actions to guarantee an uninterrupted and concentrated sleep. But note: neither coffee nor tea. Caffeine interferes with a deep slumber and attenuates one's dreams." He picked up the dream-catcher and moved it to the center of the table. Then, looking at the position of each of his guests, he adjusted the dream-catcher, turning it just so. Then he rang the bell again. A moment later Hillyer appeared. He placed a small lit candle on the table, near the dream-catcher but not too close to risk another fire; and then he dimmed the electrical lights.

"As I have said, it is unlikely you will be able to travel with me tonight. The prototype is too small. It cannot possibly contain all of our dreams, and you are unpracticed in the art and science of dreaming. But shortly *I* will vanish."

"Have you tested this before?"

"Not yet."

Filby raised an eyebrow.

"How will we know if you have traveled into the future or past?" asked the Psychologist.

After an interval, the Medical Man had an inspiration. "If you vanish, you must have gone into the past," he said.

"Why?" said the Time Traveler.

"Because I presume that you will not have moved in space, and if you traveled into the future, you would still be here all this time, since you must have traveled through this time."

"But," said I, "if he has traveled into the past, he would have been visible sitting in that chair when we came first into this room; and depending on how far he's traveled, we would have seen him last month when we were here; and the dinner before that; and so forth!"

"Serious objections," remarked Filby, with a somewhat disingenuous air of impartiality, turning towards the Time Traveler. I think we were all just playing along now, at least in part.

"Not a bit," said the Time Traveler, and, to the Psychologist: "You, think. You of all people can explain this."

The Psychologist leaned back and stared towards the ceiling in thought. "Well…," said he, "I suppose it might be presentation below the threshold, a simple point of psychology." He turned to face the table. "We will see him no more than we can see the spoke of a wheel spinning, or a bullet flying through the air. If he is traveling through time fifty times or a hundred times faster than we are, if he gets through a minute while we get through a second, the impression he'd create would of course be only one-fiftieth or one-hundredth of what he would have made if he were not traveling in time." He passed his hand through the air, sweeping it back and forth. "In fact there might be a time traveler right here, passing by us, and we would never notice!" He was obviously pleased with his theory.

We sat and stared at the vacant space in front of the Psychologist. At last the Time Traveler spoke. He did not seem quite so amused as the rest of us.

"Of course that is *not* the answer. You disappoint me, my friend. The answer is that *dream travel*, as I call it, takes place wholly outside the physical landscape of the waking realm. I had hoped that after your reading of Freud and Jung, and that upstart Perls, that *that* is what you would have said." He smiled wanly at the Psychologist before returning to the rest of us. "When I dream travel through time, I will move from waking state to the dream state first; in the dream realm I will travel psychically through space and time, invisible to all who are awake. Then once I have arrived at the right time and place, I will awaken, and return to the physical world."

"It's like traveling through a tunnel," said the Journalist. "You are outside, above ground, then you enter the tunnel and disappear, only to re-appear above ground someplace else."

The Time Traveler seemed satisfied with the Journalist's recapitulation, and he poked his lean finger towards him in a sign of concurrence. "Now," he said, "I will close the door and cut the lights." He also switched off the wireless, and when he returned to the table, he raised his arms high over his head and stretched. "Gentlemen, let me demonstrate."

And with that, our host sat down in his chair, adjusted a few of its comfort knobs, took a final sip of his Merlot, placed his hands in his lap, and closed his eyes. In the golden light of the candle, he looked rather like a painting by La Tour. After a moment of settling, we fell as silent as he. Minutes passed, and sounds we hadn't noticed before came to our attention—vague movement in another part of the house, the tick of the mantel clock, the steady breathing of our companions. Soon, however, even those sounds faded. We all watched as an absent breeze magically ruffled the feather in the web of the dream-catcher.

Moments later, our host began to snore.

We must have remained in our seats for nearly half-an-hour, watching intently as the Time Traveler slept. Finally, when it became clear he wasn't about to disappear into past or future, we rose as a group and quietly departed.

Outside the front door, the Medical Man leaned in to me to speak. "Is our friend well?" he asked.

I shook my head, at first, and then I wanted to answer in the affirmative, but I don't think I answered him at all.

9

The Time Traveler Returns

THE NEXT WEEK I arrived at the Time Traveler's home at the same moment as the Psychologist and the Silent Man. A three-axle lorry was idling in the driveway and two men were unloading a wooden crate from its bay. The container was large, at least as tall as a man, and quite a bit wider, and certainly unwieldy. The front door of the house was open, and as we approached, the Time Traveler emerged, followed immediately by Uhra.

The housemaid looked worried. "Please, sir, don't let them come in until we've laid the cardboard!"

"Of course not—but see that Hillyer has cleared a path into the library." Uhra scurried back into the house calling for the manservant.

"Careful! Careful!" the Time Traveler cautioned as the two burly men lowered the crate onto a sack barrow. He didn't seem to notice our arrival and we all stood back until the container was rolled into the house. It was at this point that the Journalist arrived.

"What's going on?" he exclaimed, and only then did the Time Traveler turn to see us.

"Welcome! Welcome!" he boomed. "You've come just in time. Come in! Come in! We'll eat, talk, and then I have something *fantastic* to show you all."

Our host beckoned us to enter, and the four of us followed. Cardboard covered the floor of the entryway, and many previously opened packages, variously small and large, were pushed towards both sides of the hall. The door to the coat room was propped open with a small statue, about a foot in height, a blue globe of the Earth balanced upon the backs of three ivory elephants, who themselves were standing on the back of a jade tortoise.

The Time Traveler saw where I was looking. "Some hold that the Earth is supported in the Heavens by elephants, and the elephants do not sink down because their feet are fixed on the back of a turtle. 'But what supports that turtle?' Why, another turtle of course! *It's turtles all the way down!* Quick stop. Won't be but a moment."

The Time Traveler popped into the coat room. The Psychologist, Journalist, and Silent Man shrugged, and I went after.

"It's in here somewhere," he said, as he began to search through a large stack of manila envelopes that dominated the surface of the room's tiny desk.

The coat room was more than a walk-in closet, but there was still little space to maneuver, and I found myself fairly well crammed in right behind our host. There were coats, of course, hanging from hooks on the walls—outerwear of nearly every kind. Overcoats and parkas, a navy blue peacoat, an old Chesterfield and a Mackintosh, a shearling, and even an ermine cloak for some reason. There were a variety of umbrellas and walking sticks. And the shoe rack contained at least half a dozen shoes and work boots. But the most significant obstacles to movement had nothing to do with our host's habiliments or haberdashery. The room was also littered with hundreds of curios and trinkets, oddities and *objets d'art*, many of them underfoot.

As the Time Traveler sorted through the stack of envelopes, I made a quick survey of those extra items he had decided to banish to this junk room. One corner was piled high with small caskets and reliquaries, one stacked upon another. They might have been jewelry boxes, or perhaps antique containers for personal correspondence. Most looked worthless, or in ill-repair, but there were others that could have been quite valuable, with gold and silver pulls. In another corner were horseshoes, broomsticks, and a rolled-up carpet. Underneath the desk were more than a dozen hand-held mirrors that looked as if they might have come from a lady's boudoir, and two colorful *matryoshkas*—Russian nesting dolls. Piled beside the desk were fist-sized stones, the kind you might see lining a walkway in a garden, or encircling a magician casting a spell.

The remaining floor was covered by an odd collection of books—I noticed *Don Quixote*, *La Biblioteca de Babel*, *The Monster at the End of This Book*, and Barthelme's *Snow White*—as well as various artistic fetishes and packets of crumbling paper, including a dirty canvas sheet, about two foot square, which held the image of a pentagram (as well as other symbols I did not recognize). There was also, quite oddly, a framed photograph of Filby wearing a clown costume.

The coat room had a single shelf above the desk. There were a multitude of hats there—an old bowler and trilby, and a boater I recognized from a trip we had taken together many years before. There were also more bundles of paper and several corrugated cardboard boxes. One was labeled Horns; another, Buildings. Finally, there were three large cups, or chalices. One was rather plain, made from battered copper, but the other two were ornate and enameled, and might have been made from more precious metals.

The Time Traveler raised a brown envelope into the air. "Ah ha!" he exclaimed, and then tilted the open sleeve into his hand. A small ring of keys slid into his palm—several mortice keys and double bits, and even an old wooden skeleton key.

"One of these should do the job nicely, I think," and he slipped the ring into his trousers pocket. Then he carefully stepped past me and back into the hallway. "This way, this way," he said.

We continued to follow him deeper into the house, sidestepping more boxes and mailing tubes. The door to the library was wide open and its frame was covered in blankets to protect the woodwork. Inside we could see Hillyer working with the two delivery men to negotiate the large crate off the two-wheeled hand truck. We all stood transfixed.

"Not now!" our host called. "Dinner first, my friends, then we will return to the library for drinks, conversation— and *amazement*."

We retreated from the threshold and followed after our host. There was a pounding of some sort coming from down the hall, and as we approached the smoking-room it grew in volume. So, too, did a pungent aroma I'd noticed upon entering the house, earthy with notes of oregano and plum. At first I'd assumed it was our dinner, and if the Medical Man were here, I was certain he'd have been able to identify the scent of each herb. But when our host opened the door and a cloud of white smoke swirled into the hallway, I realized the aroma came from a very different plant. I peered into the room. There were eight people, two just inside the entrance and six sprawled across the floor. These latter included both men and women, although their brightly colored clothes and Rapunzel-length hair made classification of sex difficult; and all of them were smoking. I identified the source of the discord, too: an LP spinning on a turntable. Rock and roll, I think. A kind of acoustic Brutalism. Thankfully, the needle had reached the end of the recording.

I recognized one of the men by the door—it was the Very Young Man from our first dinner several months before. Beside him was a sturdy gentleman in a knee-length dark coat. He had a long beard with pronounced sideburns and wore a skull cap on his head—that is, a yarmulke.

"This is our Rabbi," the Time Traveler clarified unnecessarily; and then each of us shook his hand. "Now, come, let us dine."

The Rabbi and the Very Young Man left with our host,

followed by the Silent Man, the Psychologist, and the Journalist. I was the last to leave, and the thought occurred to me that in all our years of conversation there, the smoking-room had never been quite so … smoky. I noticed also several items in the room I had not seen before, including a marra pipe (or hookah), a lava lamp, and several full-length mirrors leaning against the wall; and—this was most odd—two full-sized free-standing doors, the sort you might find on a stage for use in a theatrical production. I couldn't imagine why they were there, and wondered if similar items were inside the crate we'd just seen delivered.

Before I turned to leave the room, one of the young women on the floor waved to me. She was wearing an Apollo Mission Snoopy t-shirt cut short enough to reveal her belly button. I waved back politely, and she giggled. When I caught up with our host in the hallway, I couldn't contain my curiosity.

"Who are they?" I asked bluntly.

"In the smoking-room?" he replied, as if my question could refer to some other group of mysterious guests. "Just some friends I met this afternoon. Do you like them?"

I didn't know how to answer the question, so I remained silent. Moments later, after navigating the veritable Scylla and Charybdis of discarded boxes that littered the hallway, we'd attained the dining-room. After we'd all been seated and initial pleasantries exchanged, our host tapped spoon to the wine glass in front of him.

"Gentlemen," he began. "I have remarkable news. After several misadventures in time travel—misadventures for which I take full responsibility—I have at last untangled the weave of the problem. And tonight—tonight!—I shall be leaving you all. They say *tomorrow never comes*, yet through the application of science, mind, heart, and matter, I shall travel through the fourth dimension. I shall travel through time, I shall undo the past and change history, and I swear to you everything shall be right again!"

10

The Sentimental Machine

THERE WERE THE EXPECTED MURMURS around the table. The Psychologist leaned back and sighed. The Journalist added a gasp of exasperation. The Silent Man placed his chin upon the curl of his fist and stared intensely at our host, but whether his focus was contemplative or bemused I couldn't say. The Very Young Man danced his fingers against the tablecloth, and the Rabbi pulled gently at his beard. As for myself, I experienced an admixture of concern and excitement. Our host's continued denial of his circumstance was a source of disquiet; and yet whenever he spoke, I found it hard not to become caught in his fancy.

The fact is, the Time Traveler was one of those special men whose flights of imagination were always tethered to the ballast of intellect. As a gentleman scientist he was *sui generis*—the work of the past months was a testament to both a singular genius and an exceptional perseverance. If his flights of invention were not always successful—if they didn't quite lift off, or if they were cut short, abandoned, or even crashed—their failure, though momentarily dismaying, was always an impetus for the next attempt. The moral of the story of Icarus, he was fond of telling us, is not that man is not meant to fly so high. No, the moral is to build better wings! And if the scientific rigor of his earlier attempts—his monomaniacal focus on reason, on the systematic enterprise to build and organize his knowledge—had been supplanted now by something more ... mystical? occult? ... who was I to suggest that he did not have—if you'll pardon the self-contradiction—good reason.

Lest you suspect disingenuousness or naïveté on the part of your narrator, let me state that our friendship colored my assessment of his work. But it was not his application of reason—or heart—that I perceived in a biased fashion. No, there I was clear-headed. Rather, like the Psychologist, my partisan reaction to the man had more to do with his emotional temperament than his invention. I didn't fear for his sanity, exactly, but I feared for his psychological well-being. The loss he'd experienced would devastate anyone, and the fact that he'd had a hand in his fiancée's tragic demise made it that much worse. It is what drove him, I knew, more than any idle or intellectual curiosity. Of course I wanted to believe he might succeed in his task—for I wanted nothing more than for him to time travel, and to undo the source of his desperation and sorrow. I wanted nothing more in the whole of the world. But I also knew it was madness.

"Gentlemen," he said. "Some of you I have not seen for several months, and one of you I have met only this evening." He acknowledged the Rabbi. "It would be deceptively easy, I think, to entertain you with a nostalgic accounting of my past enterprise, but let us enjoy the meal that has been prepared for us, and while we dine I will instead expatiate upon the particulars of the present."

At that moment both Uhra and Hillyer appeared, each carrying a tray of the evening's appetizers. Our host offered wine to each of us, filling our glasses with Merlot—all except the Rabbi, who abstained.

"We know," our host began, "that there is not a single myth which has no foot in reality. Whether it's an exaggeration or distortion of a historical event, or an externalized expression of an internal conflict inherent in the human condition—such as the fear of the dark, or a yearning for meaning—myths contain at least a grain of truth, and *sometimes much more than that*."

The Psychologist raised his hand. "When you say 'myth,' what exactly do you mean?"

The Time Traveler shrugged. "I use the term broadly. For the present conversation, I include the classic myths of ancient Greece, as well as legends of the superman and the everyman, fables, even nursery rhymes. And of course all the appurtenances of modern story-telling: novels and plays and motion pictures—even television."

"Dash it, man—television!" exclaimed the Journalist.

"Myths need have only a grain of truth, so you should feel gratified I did not place your newspaper in that category."

The Journalist laughed. "Yes, very well, for that I thank you."

The Rabbi interrupted next. "Do you include religious stories as myths."

"I do, most certainly. Any story that might today seem fantastic, if not risible, to modern sensibilities. For example, in the *Odyssey* and the *Aeneid*, Aeolus is named Keeper of the Winds. He is a minor god whose story may have evolved directly from a historical account of a king who taught his people to use sails and ride the winds. That's an example of what's called euhemerism, but myths may also arise from allegory, personification, or ritual."

"That's surprisingly delicate of you, considering our present company," said the Journalist. "You have no polytheists to offend, I presume."

Our host took his point. "Very well. We are all familiar with the biblical narrative of the Exodus, and the crossing of the Red Sea."

The Rabbi nodded. "The escape of the Israelites, led by Moses, from the pursuing Egyptians."

"Go on."

"Moses points his staff towards the turbulent waters of the Red Sea, and the waters are parted by God. Once the Israelites have safely crossed, the sea closes, and the Egyptians are drowned."

The Time Traveler leaned towards the Rabbi. "Indeed, some have claimed that the parting of the Red Sea was based upon a natural event caused by a volcanic eruption. Others suggest it was a natural phenomenon known to affect large bodies of water."

"Now you're treading on more dangerous ground," the Journalist said approvingly. He turned to the Rabbi, hoping, I think, for a defense of biblical literalism; but the Rabbi gave only a small shrug.

Our host continued: "Of course it's possible the parting of the sea actually happened, more or less as described; but whether by the hand of God, or some other force, it does not matter. My point is that there is always a truth—and often a fundamental truth—in even the most incredible-seeming myth."

The Journalist chortled. "Very well. Suppose we accept your point. What then? What does this have to do with the fourth dimension?"

"Because *time travel* has been at the center of many myths. So many in fact that it's easy to overlook the possibility of its historic resonance. In fact, it's become a trope, or even a cliché, today."

"Time travel is definitely ubiquitous," agreed the Very Young Man. "It's even pop, isn't it. That Doctor fellow in the blue box seems all the rage these days."

"Exactly! The blue box. In fact, *that* is exactly what one finds at the heart of the vast majority of the myths, legends, and stories of time travel!"

There was a moment's pause, then our host continued:

"I am talking about places or special objects that by their nature bridge time and space. Of course, they've gone by many names—rifts, portals, tunnels, gates, or doors. The Time Tunnel, the Star Gate, the Guardian of Forever. A passageway in a basement, a dusty room in a museum, a circular stand of sycamore trees, a pond of still water, a mirror, a black hole, a wormhole. Even Vonnegut's chronosynclastic infundibulum, where truths of all different times come together."

The Psychologist interrupted: "So hold on now, you believe there are magical objects that—"

"Not magical. There is no magic, not in the sense that you mean. Mysteries, perhaps, or unknowns. There is no supernatural, only aspects of nature we do not yet understand. Do these objects operate following the rules of physics? Are they akin to probability waves in quantum mechanics, stretching through chords of dark matter, intersecting various points of spacetime? I haven't a clue. But it doesn't matter. The only question is: Do these special places—or *objects*—really exist?"

"And you believe they do?"

"I know they do!"

I shared my earlier insight: "So all those boxes and crates in the hallway, they held these special objects, didn't they. The mirrors and amulets and doorways I saw."

The Time Traveler shook his head. "No. Unfortunately, no. Many—most—are forgeries or scams. As you might imagine, finding a real time portal is not a trivial matter."

The Psychologist looked at me, raising his eyebrows. I could tell our host's monologue had moved into more extreme territory, but I felt the need to come to his support.

"You've succeeded, however," I said. "You've found such an object?"

The Time Traveler brightened. "You've heard of Professor Digory Kirke?"

We all looked at one another. The name sounded *vaguely* familiar.

"Not so very long ago, and not so very far from here, he planted a tree. I will not bore you with details, but countless times over many years, the tree was associated with uncanny phenomena. Its fruit cured incurable illnesses, its bark was stronger than chain-mail, and occasionally its branches would rustle wildly without benefit of a breeze. A giant storm finally felled the tree, and Kirke used the wood to build a beautiful storage container. A cabinet—"

"The crate!" the Journalist exclaimed. "Is that what we saw carried in this evening?"

The Time Traveler templed his fingers. "I think we've had our fill of food and chatter. Come with me." And with that, he rose from the table and led us back into the hallway. Again we had to step over and round the various empty boxes that I now understood to have contained objects he'd hoped were "special," and as we passed the smoking-room, the door was open, music was playing, and I was overcome once more by the aroma of hashish. The young woman who'd waved at me earlier was still there, her head in the lap of a young man who was stroking her hair. I wondered again why this group of young people was here at all.

We reached the library and saw that the cabinet had been moved into the center of the room, and space had been cleared all around it. The cabinet—it was more of a wardrobe, really—was built from carved mahogany, with ivory embellishments on its cornice and two narrow drawers at its base. It stood at least seven feet tall and was at least three feet deep, a grand piece of heirloom furniture, the kind that might have great sentimental value, handed down generation to generation. The twin doors were of a lighter wood, and each had inlaid a full-length mirror. We stared at the wardrobe, and in reflection we all stared back at ourselves.

"This is a portal not only through time, but through space as well. I haven't yet figured out how to steer the thing; I've made only preliminary tests. But I am confident I will unlock its secrets."

I wanted to ask our host what he meant by "preliminary tests," but before I could, he pulled out a set of keys, found one that worked, and opened both doors. The wardrobe was empty.

"Farewell!" he announced, and without further ado stepped up into the empty box. For a moment I had images of his stepping into a coffin, or rather a casket, at least until I saw how he had to stoop to avoid banging his head on the brass rail or becoming impaled on several hooks inside. He fumbled for a minute with the edges of each door—there were of course no handles on the inside—and then finally succeeded in pulling both doors shut. There was movement inside as he settled, then we all stood in silence, wondering what would happen next.

There was no mysterious stirring in the air. The electric lights in the room didn't flicker. The wardrobe did not change size nor shape, neither did it shimmer nor luminesce. After two minutes, there were a few more scrapes and bumps from inside the wardrobe, as if the Time Traveler couldn't get comfortable, then silence again.

We waited no more than five minutes, then finally the Psychologist stepped forward and pulled open the left-hand door. The Time Traveler was still inside, crouched down and miserable-looking. When he met our eyes, I thought for a moment he might snap at us to close the door, but instead he extricated himself from his cramped position and stepped out of the box.

"Obviously, this isn't the *original* wardrobe," he said.

Without further comment, he exited the library, and after a moment's confusion, we chased after. Before we caught him, however, he'd already disappeared down the passage to his sanctuary, the laboratory. We heard its door slam closed. We did not follow.

The Rabbi asked, "Is he a religious man?"

"How do you mean?" the Psychologist said.

"Our host. Is he an Anglican? A Catholic?"

"I'd say neither. A student of religion, perhaps. An amateur theologian. Why do you ask?"

"That wardrobe. It's C. S. Lewis, isn't it?"

I hadn't made the connection, but of course he was right.

It was from a novel, or a series of novels, about a family that travels in time and space. The Journalist nodded and the Very Young Man snapped his fingers in agreement.

For a minute or two, we all stood about uncomfortably. Then the Rabbi excused himself, as did the Very Young Man. The Journalist and the Silent Man returned to the dining-room to finish their dinner, and the Psychologist and I left the house together.

"Living too large is a kind of denial, you know—living as if every day is your last—it's another way to avoid thinking about death," the Psychologist said. "Of course, living too small—as if nothing will ever change—that's a kind of denial, too. Repeating the same thing over and over again, it's not facing the fact that time is limited, and mortality non-negotiable."

I wasn't sure what to say to that, so again I said nothing. We walked a few moments in silence until we reached the gate.

"Well, until next time," he said vaguely.

"Yes, perhaps next time he'll succeed," I answered.

We stood together a few more moments, and then we went our separate ways.

11

The Time Traveler Returns

I WAS FEELING EXCEPTIONALLY WEARY as I turned the corner towards the house in Richmond. I was recovering from a cold, that's true, and I'd learned just that afternoon of the hanging of Farzad Bazoft, a British journalist in Iraq and now a cause for national concern; but it was neither the chill nor the news that had me dragging my feet through the streets of Richmond. I'd spoken to the Time Traveler twice during the preceding week, and on each occasion he seemed to alternate between irritation and distraction. I think his failure the week before had been a serious blow, and perhaps the first time his internal resolve had faltered. In fact, it was during the second call that he mentioned T—, his fiancée, the young woman in those photographs pinned to his laboratory wall. It was only a fragmentary whisper in an unfinished sentence, but it was the first time I'd heard him speak her name since the end of October.

I was the first to arrive at his house that evening, and when Uhra led me to the dining room I couldn't help but notice the house had undergone another transformation, and this time for the better.

The boxes, crates, and flat packages had all disappeared, the hallway floor was clear of cardboard, and when I peered into the library the wardrobe was gone. A small fire was burning in the hearth, and three antique armchairs faced the gently glowing logs. The aroma that was so prevalent last week was absent as we continued down the hall towards the

69

study. Inside, the hippies were gone, as were the assorted magical mirrors and prop doors, although I noticed a precarious stack of CDs piled high next to the receiver on the credenza, and an empty shot glass on a small table beside one of the lounge chairs. When Uhra saw what I was looking at, she *tsk-tsk*'d and rushed inside to retrieve the glass. I'd imagined the Time Traveler had been in here earlier, perhaps listening to music, deep in thought, leisurely sipping his drink before the evening's guests arrived. But my optimism was dashed when Uhra said, almost under her breath, "It's getting worse, sir."

She bent down and picked up an empty liquor bottle tucked just inside the door. I hadn't noticed it there, and wondered what else I was missing.

She led me to the dining room, then went off with the glass and bottle. I checked my watch. I felt rather adrift in the house, perhaps for the first time, and lonely, and was eager for the others to arrive. The dining-table was set for five. I didn't know who had been invited except for the Psychologist, with whom I'd spoken earlier in the day. He'd expressed hesitation, though, about joining us, worried that he'd be compelled, ethically, to attend our host in a professional rather than companionable capacity. Given the circumstances surrounding our last dinner, I could understand his uneasiness.

Uhra returned presently along with Hillyer, and together they finished setting the table—napkins, silver, a vase with small white flowers, but just a pitcher of water, no wine. They placed several items into the mini-fridge beneath the buffet. As soon as they left, the feeling of being adrift returned. I thought about my conversation with the Psychologist, and then reflected on my own role in the evening's proceedings. What should be my stance to our host? Was I a friend, a confidante, an unconditional booster; or was I compelled, like the Psychologist, to be present in a more critical capacity?

I'd arrived a few minutes early, so I wasn't surprised I

was the first of the evening's visitors; however, nearly forty minutes passed before the next person appeared, and that was Filby.

"No sign of the master yet, I see," he said as he fell into the chair beside me.

I started to recount the occurrences of the previous week, but he cut me off: he'd spoken with the Journalist already.

"Is he losing his mind?" Filby asked bluntly.

I spoke before thinking, and I came to my friend's defense. "I thought he looked surprisingly healthy last week. He seems to be eating well and exercising, and—"

"I'm not talking about his physical health, blast it! I'm talking about his spirit, his mind!" Filby grunted and then poured himself a glass of water. We didn't speak for several minutes, but we knew each other well enough to understand that despite his outburst we shared a uniformity of concern. As Filby swirled the water in his glass, I felt my weariness return. He took another sip of water, then stared deep into the glass. "What do you suppose is on the menu tonight?"

I sighed. I knew he wasn't asking about cuisine. I told him I hadn't a clue, and then described the two conversations I'd had with our host earlier in the week. Before Filby could respond, the Medical Man and the Psychologist appeared. I think I rather bounded out of my chair to shake each of their hands. I was glad the Medical Man had been invited—his mind was keen and his way of thinking straightforward. Unlike Filby, whose manner was by default combative, the Medical Man's nature made him strive for harmony. Even when he might disagree with the Time Traveler, he tried to keep an open mind. Of course I was even more delighted to see the Psychologist, and as I shook his hand I felt an immediate serenity. Whether he was here in a professional capacity or not, I counted him as a close member of our circle, and one of our host's dearest friends. As we seated ourselves around the table, I was thankful we had all answered our host's call and that there would be no empty place tonight. Sometimes it felt as if we were all different parts of a single mind, and we were whole only when we were all together.

We exchanged a few minutes of pleasantries and, perhaps indirectly, some of our worries. We didn't get far, however, before we heard footsteps racing down the passage from the laboratory and the door swung open.

"Filby!" our host called out. "It's been a while!" And the Time Traveler rushed forward to embrace his friend.

Filby gave me a sideways glance as soon as the Time Traveler moved on to the Medical Man, and I knew he'd seen in just those few moments what I also observed. Our host's eyes were on fire with a kind of madness I'd not seen before. He left the Medical Man and moved on to me. He said my name, squeezed my shoulders much too hard, and finally turned to the Psychologist. They eyed one another, and our host shot out his hand. The Psychologist flinched.

"Come now!" our host said. "Don't look so tense! *Time* is the enemy, and I'm going to beat it. I'm going to save her. You just watch." He commanded everyone sit, and we all obeyed. "But first—a toast!"

The Time Traveler avoided the water on the table and instead moved on to the small liquor cabinet. "*Tomorrow, and tomorrow, and tomorrow,*" he mumbled. "*A walking shadow— heard no more.*" He extracted a tall bottle of Kentucky Vintage bourbon, poured himself a glass, and brought the bottle back to the table. "Physician, help thyself!" he commanded. "And *that* is this evening's toast!"

He knocked back the first shot and then poured himself another, then finished that just as quickly. He pounded the glass to the table and then examined each of us in turn. His eyes narrowed and he seemed to be sizing us up—but for what purpose I had no idea. When our eyes met, I felt as if he was hoping to pry open the mirror to my soul. It was, to say the least, uncomfortable.

The Time Traveler returned to the buffet. No one said anything as he pulled a small platter from the bottom shelf, peeled off its cover of plastic wrap, and put it directly into the microwave. No one said anything as he set the timer, nor for the sixty seconds the machine hummed and whirred and the scent of melted butter and sugar and cinnamon filled the room. And no one said anything when the bell finally went off and our host carried the plate to the dining-table and set it before us. There were ten biscuits—they looked like Jammie Dodgers—each perfectly round with a dab of dark red fruit in its center. Steam wafted into the air.

"Ah," he said, laughing. "I see you're all eyeing my latest creation with suspicion. What can they be! The ultimate secret to time travel? Will these six disks shortly obtain the mass of Neptune?" He poured himself a third drink, but didn't bring it to his lips, rather he used it as a blunt pointer, gesturing into the air as he spoke, the amber liquid sloshing over the rim of the glass. "I won't bore you with details," he said as he circled the table. "Because of course *they're just biscuits*, you fools! For eating! Eat them!" he commanded, and he seized one from the plate and took an angry bite for himself.

The weariness I'd felt upon arrival returned and was now tinged with a certain hopelessness. In fact, I was dumbfounded, and looking round the table it was apparent the feeling was shared. I thought about poor Uhra and whatever behavior she must have witnessed—and endured—throughout the week.

The Time Traveler planted himself in front of me, drink in hand, and then fumbled a few times to reach with that same hand into an inner pocket of his jacket. He cursed repeatedly, then gave up, finished the drink and set it on the table. Then he tried again. This time he was able to pull out a small stack of cards. I thought at first they were playing cards—or tarot cards, perhaps? It wouldn't have surprised me. But I was wrong on both counts. He turned to the Medical Man first and peeled off the label at the top of the stack and—*slap!*—stuck it to his chest. The Medical Man's eyes went wide. We all took a closer look, and yes, indeed, it was a name tag with the name of the Medical Man written in large-tip black marker. The Time Traveler proceeded round the room and slapped a name tag on each of us. His actions could not have been more surprising—or worrisome—or infuriating.

"There!" he said when he'd finished. "Now I know each of you, and each of you know one another." He surveyed us again, cursorily this time, and a cryptic smile burst upon his countenance: "But for how long, do you think? How long?"

12

The Anti-mechanist Machine

THE TIME TRAVELER paced the room, hands behind his back. He wasn't completely steady on his feet, and for the first time I detected a slurring of words as he launched into this evening's esoteric lecture.

"I admit to making some small mistakes in the past. Who hasn't?" he began. "Physics, mind, relativity, historicity, quantum mechanics, Dreamtime, geometry, light speed, imagination, heart—I've explored them all. Every cursed one. But they're useless—*useless* without the most important factor." He turned on us, tilting forward as if daring us to speak. "It's spirit, of course. The human spirit!"

He reached for the glass he'd placed in front of me but misjudged the distance between finger and glass and sent it off the table's edge.

"God damn it!" he snapped, and kicked after the tumbler.

The Psychologist stood and started to speak, but the Time Traveler spoke over him: "There are stories, treatises, scrolls, histories, fables—too many to mention, but I have catalogued them all. Every last one. I had Hillyer xeroxing for hours. Hours and hours. The laboratory is overflowing, come see! The walls are covered with notes—you'll see. Documents, diagrams, charts, pins, pictures, postcards, letters...." He seemed to drift off for a moment. "No matter! Come, come, I must show you my catalogue!"

We all looked at one another. The Psychologist sat back down.

"No? *No?* What is wrong with all of you!" He lurched towards us, fists clenched, and I thought for a moment he might strike out. "The Internet? Have you all used the Internet? Can I get a *yes* to that at least? That massive network, moving packets of information from source to destination, hopping from one router to the next like rabbits or fleas. Like waves in the ocean, a ripple of information that passes through the physical substrate of the sea. Think about it! The *wave travels* but the *molecules of water do not!* Exactly like the spirit in our bodies, the soul that migrates from host to host, eon to eon, reborn, rebirthed, transmigrated, reincarnated—you see?"

Not one of us spoke. In fact, not one of us moved. The Medical Man was holding a biscuit near his mouth, and it had been held there, frozen, for the duration of the entire speech. The Psychologist and Filby both held water glasses, hands trembling.

Our host continued, oblivious I think to the stunned response his fervent allocution had thus far received. He began to pace back and forth.

"The ancient art of soul travel, it is called. In the Saṃsāra doctrine of cyclic existence, it's the cycle of death and rebirth. In the Greek histories, Pythagoras, Socrates, and Plato—he who saw the soul of Orpheus change into a swan!—it's *metempsychosis*. Schopenhauer and Gödel talk about it endlessly. Endlessly! Even Joyce repeats it in *Ulysses*—metempsychosis metempsychosis *blah blah blah*. An intellectual strike against the fallacy of imitative form!"

The Time Traveler found himself in front of the liquor cabinet again. He fumbled around for a moment, but then seemed to forget why he was there and turned back to us. He pointed a lean finger in our direction, and then changing his hand into the shape of a pistol, he pointed the barrel to his own temple.

"My mistake has been to think that I can travel backward in time *with my body*. Boom!" His hand jerked from his head.

"But my body—the molecules and atoms, the electrons, protons, positrons, quarks—all with physical substance—can't *go* anywhere. When we are born, our souls are locked into the physical substrate of our bodies, and our bodies are fixed in four dimensions. We can't physically go back in time because our bodies are already there. This is the fundamental paradox of time travel. Ah, but the soul! The soul has no mass, no weight. Twenty-one grams—bullshit! No, it is weightless, without mass, and once liberated from the body *it may be unstuck in time.* Blow on it and it moves, as the Spirit of God moved upon the face of the waters. Are you beginning to see?"

The Time Traveler returned to the table. "I've solved it. Damn it, this time I've solved it!" He sat in the empty seat between Filby and the Medical Man. "I've solved it!" he repeated, and he slammed the flat of his palm against the dining-table.

"Come on," the Time Traveler said. "Join hands! Damn you all, join hands!" He reached out to his neighbors.

The Medical Man was first, cautiously taking the Time Traveler's left hand in his right. Filby followed, taking the Time Traveler's right hand in his left, and we all did likewise with our neighbors. I don't think any of us knew what else to do.

"Is this to be a séance?" the Psychologist asked, and I realized this was the first comment any of us had made since the Time Traveler began his raving.

Filby spoke next: "Perhaps you should have invited our friend the Journalist this week. Surely this is the kind of lark his readers would like to read about."

Our host ignored both comments.

"When a soul travels through time, it has identity but no substance, and no sense until it is incarnated into a body with the senses—sight, smell, hearing, taste, and touch. Soul travelers take tours in other people's lives. It's a kind of lifetime machine, or anti-mechanist machine, where anyone anywhere who has ever lived can act as a receptacle, a destination for the soulful time traveler, if you'll pardon the expression. And once in the past, once a soul has inhabited a four-dimensional body in time and space, then *that* time and space will become the present! It's how I can change history. It's how I can change *her* story!"

"Are you talking about possession?" the Medical Man asked.

The Time Traveler waved him off. "No. Well, *yes*. But no, I will not chronicle the long history of possession. All you need to understand is that not all spirits are evil, and not all souls untethered move through time. Yet it can be done! I will guide my soul into a body in the past, and then open my eyes into the eyes of the host, and fill all its senses, and I will be possessed with the body as the body is with me. There may be some confusion of the sense of self, hence the need for name tags—it's a precaution—but then I shall return."

The Time Traveler tilted his head back and briefly closed his eyes. "'Our two souls therefore,'" he whispered, "'which are one, though I must go, endure not yet a breach, but an expansion, like gold to airy thinness beat.'"

I could see the Medical Man stir uncomfortably in his seat.

"Now, by holding hands we close a Kirlian circuit. We shall all of us imagine a single time and place—and person. An *event*. You know of that which I speak. Then I will soul travel to each of you in turn. Proof of concept. The damn pudding. I will visit each of you in time! Shut your eyes," he commanded, "and observe the entirety of the world through your third eye, the invisible eye, right above and between the eyebrows—*the spiritual eye*. Picture that place and time—then close that eye, too."

The Time Traveler closed his eyes, and the rest of us looked at one another. Finally, the Medical Man lowered his head in resignation and closed his eyes. The Psychologist was next, shaking his head. Filby and I looked at one other. I could tell he thought this ludicrous, and I could not disagree; then he shrugged and closed his eyes, too. I waited a moment, and I closed my own.

After a moment of silence, the Time Traveler began to speak. It was a mumble at first, but shortly turned into a recitation, or rather an incantation. I would not have been surprised if it was Latin, or Greek, or even an esoteric language of the Druids. In fact, I would have preferred any of those to what soon became apparent—it was nothing more than a mantra of gibberish. I felt the fingers of those on either side of me—the Medical Man and the Psychologist—tighten as the Time Traveler's chant began, and once it ended I struggled to keep my eyes closed, especially when I felt a certain unequivocal chill pass through the room. The silence of our circle, however, was soon broken.

"I'm back!" the Time Traveler exclaimed.

I opened my eyes. Apparently I was the last to do so, for everyone else was already fixated on our host. "Filby," he said, reading Filby's name off the tag on his chest before looking at his face. "I saw you first, in the side yard. You were smoking."

Filby said: "I am in the side yard often. What are you talking about?"

"You were smoking."

Filby nodded. "I do that quite a bit, too."

The Time Traveler shook his head. "It was *evening*. It was *October*. You'd smoked less than half of the cigarette—Bond Street—and you stubbed it out against the lower wall."

Filby started to speak again, but the Time Traveler scuppered his rebuttal. He pushed back from the table and stood, pointing to the Psychologist next and speaking his name.

"*You* were standing in the library, your fingers brushing over the spines of the books on the high shelf. You were thinking about Annabel Lee, your wife. You were with our friend"—he pointed at me—"and you had come to the library to look for consolation in words. For me? For yourself? You pulled down a volume of Donne. Then paged through it until you found 'A Valediction: Forbidding Mourning,' a poem you know well. It seemed a fine choice, and it served a dual purpose."

He turned to look at me. "*You* followed him down the stairs. He had mentioned wanting to find something to read, but you suspected the library was at least as much a retreat as a reconnoiter. It certainly was for you."

Neither the Psychologist nor I responded before he turned to the Medical Man. "And *you* pronounced her," the Time Traveler said. "You touched her forehead, as if you wanted to see if she was running a fever. She reminded you of your daughter. You bit your lip at the chill of her skin. Then—"

Filby interrupted: "Stop it! This is monstrous!"

The Medical Man stood up and in a rare flash of anger raised a fist: "It's absurd! You were there with me. This isn't time travel, this is memory! What is wrong with you!"

The Psychologist added softly, "Indeed, my friend, this seems all quite disturbed."

The Time Traveler twitched as if administered a shock; and if anything, the gentle tone of the Psychologist seemed to ignite something in our host. His face turned red. "Not one of you understands! You're all fools! Ignorant fools!" He grabbed the back of his chair and flung it across the room. It crashed against the buffet.

"Don't you see? *I did it.* I traveled backward in time. Just now. It worked—it finally worked. I saw all of you, through each of your eyes. And—and I saw *her*...!" He turned his back to us, body shaking. I feared violence might come next. He spun round. "Next time I will change everything! I will change everything! Your wife! Your daughter! I can change it all! I saw her, oh dear God *I saw her!*"

The Time Traveler fell to his knees. He began to howl, both hands pulling at his hair.

We quickly left our seats and encircled our host. "We're here, now," the Psychologist said. "We're all right here, right now." The Medical Man rang the bell and moments later Hillyer arrived, assessed the situation, and retreated, to return moments later with Uhra. Together they helped their master up, and then led him out of the dining room.

We stood around awkwardly for a minute or two, and in silence, and then the Medical Man poured himself another glass of water. The Psychologist went straight to the liquor cabinet and poured something stronger. I returned to my seat, but the others did not.

"He could have seen the mark of ash on the stone wall later and surmised the rest," Filby said.

"So you *were* in the garden?"

"When she was pronounced? Yes, of course. But of course I was. That should be no surprise. I am out there often. Too often. It's a simple deduction."

The Psychologist added, "As he must have done concerning the library, seeing the John Donne on the desktop. I don't think I replaced it that evening when the nurse called us back. He saw it later and put two and two together."

"And of course I was there with him," the Medical Man concluded. "Right beside him, in fact." He grunted and then finished his drink. "I have tried to keep an open mind. I have. And then all this balderdash. There is simply no such thing as time travel. The past is the past. I tell you—our friend has lost the plot."

13

The Time Traveler Returns

ON SATURDAY EVENING, I received an email from the Time Traveler apologizing for his behavior at our previous gathering. He said he'd been inconsiderate to his guests and "particularly unfair" to me. I replied without hesitation, letting him know that an apology was unnecessary and that I did not feel treated unfairly in any way. I told him I understood the hard position he'd found himself in over this past year, and that I—all of his friends, really—wanted nothing more for him than to find a peace that we knew had thus far eluded him. I did not hear from him again until Wednesday, when a second email arrived. This time the message was addressed also to the Physician and the Psychologist, inviting all three of us to his house the following evening *aut delectare aut prodesse*—"to instruct or delight." (This, from Horace's *Ars Poetica*, which I took to be a good sign; although I realized that even if we accepted his offer, it would be our smallest gathering yet.)

I telephoned the Physician first and he suggested the three of us meet thirty minutes before the proposed dinner on Thursday, again at the Bad Wolf in Brentford; and so we did. Our conversation was unusually frank, but when the three of us arrived together at the house in Richmond at half-past seven, we felt confident we would present a unified front to our host.

Mrs. Watchett answered the door and led us into the drawing room where the fire was already blazing in the hearth. She said dinner would be served at eight and that our host would be down shortly to join us for a drink. She unlocked the liquor cabinet—an unexpected turn, considering the overindulgence of the previous week—and stressed that he bid us all to help ourselves. To be honest, the idea of another drink before the arrival of our host was not unappealing. "A bit more Dutch courage," mooted the Physician, and we all three approached the bar. The Physician poured himself a neat whisky; the Psychologist, a gin with a whisper of vermouth; and I satisfied myself with a gin and tonic. Since we'd spoken at length before arriving, we were sparing in our conversation now, and instead savored our drinks and let them do their work on us. Our host arrived before we finished the first round.

"Salutations," he said upon entering the room. He spread his arms as he approached, and I could see immediately he was not the same man who had raved and ranted at us the week before. More relaxed, slower and easier in his movements, and certainly not intoxicated; and if his smile was a little tight, it did not appear forced. "Please, sit." He indicated the armchairs that had been placed in front of the fire. The Physician moved to the chair nearest the Time Traveler, the Psychologist beside him, and I at the far end.

"You are my closest friends," he began. "My most trusted. All this"—he swept his hand easily through the air, a gesture that might have been meant to encompass the furnishings of the room or the entirety of the world—"is vanity. 'Ill at ease under indifference as tenderness is under a love which it cannot return,'" he whispered. "It is surface, not substance, and none of it means much to me. We four, here and now, stationed as we are before the warmth of the fire, with beating hearts in our breasts counting time—this is important. Being together. *This* is Life."

We all nodded, though I doubt any of us knew precisely the course our host had set for the evening's conversation.

"I have had a hard week," he admitted, and we all nodded again; although, truly, he had been struggling for far longer than that, and we could see his situation weighed on him. He placed his hands in his lap, one atop the other. "Nevertheless, I must apologize. Our last dinner was disappointing. I was overcome by the darker demons of my nature, and I do not think I have ever felt such rage. Rage at a universe that could destroy such a tender and beautiful flower, and that would have my hand be the instrument used to rip her from the earth. Rage at her acceptance of mortality and my easy complicity in her demise. Rage at all of you, too, for supporting such a drastic ending. And of course rage at my inability, time and again, to undo this tragedy. What kind of universe must we inhabit that can seem so malevolent—or worse, so indifferent—to the human condition?" He laughed. "As I said: a hard week."

The Physician placed a hand on our host's shoulder.

"Thank you. Really, all of you for your perseverance and companionship. I know none of this is easy. And yet—suffering is not without its own reward, is it not."

The Time Traveler stood and made his way to the liquor cabinet. As I watched him rise in stages, carefully supporting himself on the arms of the chair, I could tell he was wearied, and I knew that he knew it, too. When he returned, I was relieved to see he'd poured himself a cranberry juice. He reseated himself.

"This has been a week both exhausting and laborious, as I have said, but it has not been a week without progress—or revelation. I realize I cannot go on as I have. I am sure you understand."

All of us were quick to concur.

"Since we were last together, I have made an overall reassessment of my circumstance. First, I have considered my attempts to travel through time. I have reread my notes and equations, and inspected every prototype." The Time Traveler smiled. "Well, at least those prototypes which didn't self-immolate, or wind up deep beneath what was once the foundation of this house."

"Indeed!" I replied, and the others joined in with encouraging remarks as well, all of us relieved to hear the wry and self-effacing humor we'd long associated with our friend, but which had been so absent of late.

"Second, I have been thinking about the past. In particular, the events surrounding the twenty-fifth of October. And third, I have been thinking about the future."

"You have been busy!" the Physician said approvingly. "That is a comfort. Putting the past behind you, facing the future, keeping occupied. I wholeheartedly approve!"

The Psychologist jumped in. "I agree: this is excellent progress! Getting everything out. Confronting the events of this past year and your response to them. Difficult, but admirable."

"There are no short-cuts in these matters," said I. "But we are all pleased that you are looking at the big picture."

Our host nodded. "Yes—in fact, without the thorough understanding this reassessment provided, I could never have completed another design."

"Hold on—*a new machine?*"

"You mean to say you've created another prototype? You are still determined to travel in time?"

Our host leaned forward. "I can imagine what you are all thinking—the madness, the futility—but everything is different now. I have committed *everything* to this undertaking." His voice dropped to nearly a whisper as he made his petition: "I beg that you will indulge me once more."

Almost as one, we raised our drinks to our lips, deliberately inhibiting our ability to respond as we each pondered our host's request. The Physician was the first to put down his glass and speak. "You know I support you in every way, and if you have something to demonstrate this evening, I will of course bear witness. But, my friend, to be frank, and as a doctor, and after seeing you tonight, and listening to you now—well, listen to me. I worry about your physical health. You *must* convalesce. Promise me that after we finish this evening—after you tell us whatever it is you wish to say, and show us whatever you wish to show us— you will give yourself a chance to recuperate."

We had rehearsed much of this speech earlier in the pub, and our host made no response at first, despite the worthy delivery by the Physician.

The Psychologist took a deep breath and spoke next: "You have said we are your closest friends, and of course we are. That's why I've kept my distance, why I haven't interfered with what you've needed to do. I trusted in your ability to recover—in your own way and on your own terms. But I agree with what the doctor has said: you need rest. You do not seem well. You seem mentally exhausted. Promise me, also, please, that you will rest."

"You must let us take care of you," I added quickly. "It is our duty and pleasure—as your best friends—to help you find peace."

Our host finished his drink; then he smiled. Even before he spoke, I could tell he had heard what we had said and that it had touched him. "True peace, I fear, is the undiscovered country, but I will settle for rest. After tonight—when all of this is done, when after these past six days of creation I demonstrate to you my latest invention— I assure you I will get some well-deserved rest."

The Time Traveler stood, and we watched as he returned to the bar and poured himself another drink. I'm sure none of us missed that it was whisky this time. For several moments he seemed to contemplate the glass in his hand, then he said:

"I think tonight we shall skip our formal dinner. Come, refill your glasses and I'll have Mrs. Watchett bring us bread and meat and cheese. We will stay here this evening."

I could see the disappointment on the Physician's face— he more than any of us loved a fine meal. But our host tapped his fingernail against the bottle of whisky, twice, and the pings were sufficient to catch the Physician's attention. He came to his feet, and we all joined him at the bar. Our host rang the bell, and after Mrs. Watchett came and left with her instructions, he returned to his chair to begin the next chapter of the evening's discourse.

"Let's start with a review of my previous efforts to build a mechanism, or harness, capable of transporting a person backward and forward in time." He looked at the Psychologist. "I suppose, my friend, that you might advise I should avoid the term 'post-mortem,' and yet it is particularly apt, is it not?"

The Psychologist had by this time returned to her seat with her martini replenished. She didn't answer our host directly, but raised the glass in a salute of friendly, if not enthusiastic, participation. We all realized we were back in a situation over which we had limited influence.

"Very well, I shall begin. Excuse the brevity, but I do not wish to bore you with details...."

Between sips of whisky and the occasional gesticulation, our host spent the next thirty to forty minutes recapitulating his efforts to travel through time—though I suspect the disquisition was as much for his benefit as ours. I would not say the discourse bored me, although it seemed that there could not have been many details of his narrative left out. Fortunately, as I finished my second drink and began my third, Mrs. Watchett returned with the first tray of cold cuts and cheeses, else I might have become quite overcome by the effects of the alcohol. The Physician and the Psychologist asked several clarifying questions along the way, and I ventured one or two myself, and by the end I think we all felt confident that our host was as lucid as ever. He may have been physically weak, and his emotional state was far from ideal, but one could not doubt the intellectual force of the man. He stood and fixed himself a sandwich of roast beef and cheddar, then returned to his seat in front of the fire before continuing with the second item that had preoccupied him during the week.

"The past is never easy to face," he began. "The happiest childhood is reduced to imperfect and fragmentary memories, or a nostalgia for cheap toys and trinkets. Even yesterday is thrown into the oubliette of time. You may hear its dwindling echoes, even as you clutch after whatever's left behind—jewelry, postcards, photographs...." He looked into his open hands and sighed. "The human condition is one of disheartening events—none of which can be said with certainty to be right or wrong, or better or worse, because no one has ever gone back, no one has had a do-over, no one can know what a *no* might have accomplished in place of the *yes*. 'Shall I part my hair behind? Do I dare to eat a peach?' Our lives are not a scientific experiment. There are no repeatable procedures, no opportunity for logical analysis of results. There is no distinction in life between an experimental sample and a control. And yet we do understand *at an intuitive level* something about the quality of the choices we make. And so we look back over our lives and long for things to have been different."

The Time Traveler took another sip of his drink. Swirled the whisky in his glass.

"In this sense, life is neither feast nor spectacle, as George Santayana has said; it is a predicament. And finding a method to travel backward in time to change the past is elusive. Therefore I have made mistakes which can *never* be corrected."

The Psychologist raised her hand and was about to speak, but the Time Traveler shook his head.

"Not yet," he said. "I want to talk first about that night. Only you three, I think, understand what happened. Was it right or wrong that Tamara fell ill? Was her delirium and pain for the best? Was her wish for surcease a sin? Was my willingness to help set her free a crime? When I held the cup to her lips...."

Again he drifted off, and I knew exactly what images were being painted in his imagination. Recognizing that, and hearing him utter her name for only the second time in many months, I felt a chill run through me.

"Who can say what is right or wrong, or where morality ends and reality begins? But you must agree—you must have no doubt—that *it was the worst outcome possible.* Any other would be preferred!"

He took another drink. His eyes were open but he was far away; and this time I did not know where he had gone. When he returned, he smiled wanly and began what was more narrative than memoir. He went through that dreadful night minute by minute, action by action, part eulogy, panegyric, and confession. It was the first time he'd talked about it so openly with any of us. Half an hour passed, and his story concluded, he lowered his head. His sorrow and grief were in the air all around us, like a heavy fog, but I could also sense a certain relief in our host, perhaps for having just let the story out. We were silent for several moments, then the Psychologist spoke:

"We are—I am sure I may speak for all of us—so terribly sorry for your loss. And I know all of us who were present during that day—Filby, myself, your good friend here, *everyone*—offer you our deepest condolences."

"Thank you." He looked up, eyes glistening in the firelight. "Now, please bear with me. I have one last thing to say. I have spoken of my work and the past. Now I must discuss the future. Although to say that I have been 'thinking about the future' is a bit of misdirection. In fact, what I have been thinking about is *escape.*"

"Escape from the past, you mean?"

"The past *and* the present. Anything to get away from *here.*" He jerked his hand through the air, then he looked at each of us in turn. When his eyes fell on me, he resumed: "But the more I thought about it, the more ludicrous the idea seemed. Understand: I may have the means to travel forward to the future—even if at the meager speed of life— but is *escape* actually possible? This question filled me with foreboding. Simply put, if we can't change the past, then we are condemned to live with it in the present. And if it is in the present, it will be dragged with us into the future. That is to say, if we can't go back and change a word in the book of our life, if what's done is done, then we can only keep going, adding word after word, writing chapter after chapter—with no hope to rewrite, to change, to improve our story. The horror of the past is always with us. And so if the past is a prison, I realized, so is the future. There is no escape. No matter how far I fly, my grief will catch up with me."

There followed an uncomfortable silence, and I recall staring into the remains of my gin and tonic to avoid meeting the gaze of our host.

"That sounds rather hopeless," the Physician said at last.

"Hopeless?" He laughed. "No. Just the opposite! This realization—it's swept away the darkness. It's opened my eyes. Understand: if I cannot time travel to the past to rewrite history to save my sweet Tamara, and if I cannot time travel to the future to outrun this grief, then only one path remains. By the simple process of elimination, I must time travel *to the present.*"

14

The Presentiment Machine

"TIME TRAVEL TO THE PRESENT?" the Physician exclaimed. "You're talking nonsense again!"

"You aren't listening. I have told you that I would synthesize my approaches. I have done just that."

The Psychologist groaned. "So you have not given up the idea of traveling to the past or future," she said.

"Of course not, but that misses the point. Recall, I spoke of the geometry of spacetime, of our three dimensions and the fourth—time. But now we must look at it a different way. Rather than thinking of Cartesian coordinates and of four dimensions, we might think of Eratosthenian coordinates—the latitude and longitude used to mark one's location on Earth. What if we extend that to include time?"

"I don't see how that makes any difference," said the Physician.

"No, not yet. I spoke also of special and general relativity—remember?—of the speed of light and the effect of mass on spacetime. You remember the uncertainty principle? How, at a quantum level, eliminating uncertainty about the position of a particle maximizes uncertainty about its momentum, and eliminating uncertainty about its momentum maximizes uncertainty about its position."

"Well, yes," the Physician begrudged.

"—And that until you observe a quantum event, a probability distribution assigns probabilities to all possible values of position and momentum, but—"

"Now you've lost me!" the Physician exclaimed.

"He's talking about Schrödinger's cat," I interrupted, and the Time Traveler grinned. I'm not sure how that particular detail came to me, but it was one of the few features of the uncertainty principle with which I was familiar. (Well, "familiar" may be overstating it.)

"Quite right," the Time Traveler confirmed. "It's a classic thought experiment in physics. More precisely, it's Erwin Schrödinger's evocation of a problem he saw in the Copenhagen interpretation of quantum mechanics."

"You better remind me," said the Psychologist. "I've heard of it, too, but vaguely."

I gave it a go: "There's a cat in a box, but you don't know if it's dead or alive until you actually look inside the box. And—" I sighed. "Well, I suppose that's really the extent of my knowledge."

The Time Traveler laughed again. "You're close enough. There's a cat, a flask of poison, and a device triggered by a quantum event. If the event occurs, the flask is shattered, releasing the poison and killing the cat."

"Killing the cat!" the Physician cried.

"It's a hypothetical cat only. A hypothetical cat that may be simultaneously both alive and dead, a state known as a quantum superposition. Like the subatomic particles whose position and momentum are in multiple states until they are frozen—made real—upon measurement, the cat is simultaneously alive and dead. Yet, when one looks in the box, one sees the cat either alive or dead, not both alive and dead. This raises the question of when exactly quantum superposition ends and reality collapses into one possibility or the other."

"It's all a bit mind-boggling and unreal."

Our host nodded. "The unreal made real, yes. And it suggests another, even more intriguing, possibility. Or rather, a probability. I will not bore you with details, but it's conceivable that the 'reality collapse'—the collapse of the eigenstate—is only a *subjective* phenomenon. That is, it's local to the observer. What if the universal waveform—and every probable outcome—is equally valid and there is no wave function collapse. All possible outcomes are realized. Yes, the cat may be dead *here*, but alive *somewhere else*. And so time is not merely a straight line in the fourth dimension; time is a many-branched tree, wherein every possible outcome is realized. It suggests that there is a large—perhaps *infinite*—number of universes."

"That's even more mind-boggling!"

"Yes, which is why we might imagine that traveling along latitude is akin to traveling through time, going from the beginning of time at the South Pole to the end of time at the North Pole—"

"Well, that's easy enough."

"—And traveling along longitude, circling around the globe, is traveling *perpendicular to time*. That is, to other timelines."

"That's nonsense!"

"It is not. Multiple timelines have been hypothesized not only in physics, but also in cosmology, astronomy, religion, philosophy, psychology, music, and every kind of literature. Parallel universes, parallel dimensions, modal realism, the metaverse, separate realities, alternate realities—they are all self-contained planes of existence, co-existing with our own. And with each moment that passes, with each quantum event, the tree of time is constantly branching—"

"Hold on, man! No one in his right mind would give this credence."

"Hardly! The idea is *everywhere*. Even Plato reflected on the idea of parallel realities. Ancient Hindu mythology, in texts such as the Puranas, acknowledge an infinite number of universes, each with its own gods. Heaven, Hell, Olympus, and Valhalla are all alternate planes of existence. Alexander the Great wept over worlds innumerable, and that he was not yet lord of one! Is Hugh Everett mad? Is

Bryce DeWitt? The idea fairly litters the literary genre, too. There's Andre Norton's *The Crossroads of Time,* Philip K. Dick's *The Man in the High Castle,* David Gerrold's *The Man Who Folded Himself,* Isaac Asimov's 'The End of Eternity,' and most recently Sergey Lukyanenko's *Rough Draft.* In fact, Murray Leinster's 'Sidewise in Time' is the work from which I drew the analogy to latitude and longitude. There have been plays and movies, of course, from *Doppelgänger* to *Donnie Darko,* from *Fatherland* to *Run Lola Run—*"

The Physician threw his hands in the air. "My friend, you are a brave man! That you have survived these past months without Tamara is remarkable. But this! I am afraid this time you have gone too far. These repeated attempts. These repeated failures. Can't you see? You are torturing yourself."

"A coward dies a thousand times before his death, but the valiant taste of death but once?"

"Exactly, man! You must face facts. Nothing *might* have been. What is, is. The world may seem a garden of forking paths, but really there is only one path we take. There are no alternatives. The one branch we're on is the only branch. This dream of yours—of time travel—it's a fantasy. Accept what is before you. Quantum reality, the multiverse, time travel to the present—it's balderdash!"

"But that's just it. In an infinity of timelines, the brave man dies just as often as the coward. The only questions are *when* and *where* and *how.* There is somewhere and somewhen—in another timeline—where my sweet Tamara is still alive. I know this is true. Where on this day—*this* very day—she still breathes. In fact, there are millions of those timelines—billions! An infinitude! That I am just so unlucky to have landed in *this* particular timeline—well, that is something I shall correct!"

The Psychologist placed her hand on the Physician's shoulder before he could react again, and she shook her head. He sank back into his chair.

"You see, I have been exceedingly close to success in all

my attempts," the Time Traveler continued. "Closer than you might imagine. In fact, I was able to modify my first prototype to take into account quantum decoherence in order to slide not along a singular axis of time, but across multiple timelines parallel to our own. Crossing timelines, it turns out, is no different from moving through the hours of the day, or the days of the year. And I don't need to travel far. Really—think of it!—I need only move far enough to a timeline where a single *yes* of hers becomes a *no*, to one in which Tamara decides not to kill herself. One in which, dear God, I do not convince her that it's a good idea!"

The Time Traveler finished his appeal and we all sat stunned before him. Finally, the Psychologist spoke: "So this is how you plan to improve your life? Change the past and escape the future?"

"You misunderstand. Forget the past and future. You drive it sideways, from one timeline to another. Grief is love imprisoned, unable to touch the source of its affection, and so without Tamara, I have no choice but to end this life— to leap off this necrotic branch and find another!"

The Time Traveler then stood and left the room, and again we could hear his slippers shuffling down the hallway towards the laboratory. He returned a moment later with his latest mechanism held in his arms. He placed the machine on one of the room's octagonal tables, and then moved both table and machine nearer the fire, so we might all have a better look. The new mechanism appeared almost exactly like the prototype he had shown us that first evening: a glittering metallic framework, scarcely larger than a mantel clock. There was ivory in it, and some colorful crystals. There was also a separate mirrored band, similar to the second prototype he'd shown us, and this he placed upon his head like a crown. He then pulled several items from his pocket. The dream-catcher was attached to a loop of cord, and this he hung around his neck. The small white disk, about the size of a penny, he pressed into his forehead. Finally, he peeled off a rectangular sticker from its backing and slapped a name tag against his breast. "This device merges all that I have learned—from spacetime geometry to relativistic travel, from quantum physics to the power of dreams. I shall now slip away. Not into the past or the future, but the present. An *alternate* present."

The Psychologist seemed about to speak, but changed her mind. Really, what was there to say? Then the Time Traveler put forth his finger towards the lever. "No," he said. "I want you to participate. Lend me your hand." And turning to the Psychologist, he took her hand in his own and told her to put out her forefinger.

We all saw the lever turn. The engine started.

"Farewell!"

The action of the mechanism was much as it had been that first night, although this time it did not sputter. There was a flash of light from the band atop his head, and a rush of warm air in the room. The white disk on his forehead glowed slightly for a moment, like a third eye of wisdom, then dimmed into blackness. The little machine began to tremble, then to hum—much like a purring cat. Then it became more musical, like a slow draw across the strings of a cello, until it was replaced by a human voice—a woman's voice, whispering. Before I could make out the words, the Time Traveler jumped to his feet, knocking back his armchair. He stumbled away from the table.

"Has it really worked?" he asked. His face had gone white and he was staring wide-eyed at each of us, as if we were somehow suddenly unknown to him. The black disk fell from his forehead and the time machine went silent. *"Has it worked?"* he asked again. He jerked his head round the room, as if to make sure he knew where he was. Then he turned back to us, gibbering.

"My God! *You*—and *you* and *you*! I've done it! I've done it!"

15

The Time Traveler Returns

THERE WAS NO INVITATION from our host to dine with him the next Thursday, although he was on all our minds, and a number of his former guests exchanged text messages throughout the week. Filby insisted "time travel is a fool's errand, a selfish and self-defeating illusion." The Editor said our host was "leading himself down the primrose path, and trying to take us with him." The Physician repeatedly typed "balderdash!" The Provincial Mayor said the very idea of time travel was "politically problematic and personally dangerous." The Bishop quoted Kipling. And the Therapist insisted our host was undergoing a "reaction formation." She thought he didn't believe in time travel any more than we did, but was desperate to assuage his own guilt by *doing something*.

Since none of us shared an opinion that was controversial or contrary to that of the others, we were preaching to our own choir; and whatever we ranted and raved on social media was probably not so different from the "reaction formation" of our host—an effort to assuage our own guilt by doing something, however pointless.

By Monday afternoon we began brainstorming solutions, which was an improvement—although I don't know why it took us so long to get there. The Therapist and the Physician shared lists of half a dozen medical and psychological professionals they felt might offer support to our host. The Imam offered contact information for various religious men and women of different faiths. The Very

Young Woman proposed sending the Time Traveler to a Zen Buddhist dojo for meditation instruction. Filby had the idea of moving our friend to the extra room in his home in Kensington. The Editor knew a program at Oxford's Counselling Service for dealing with grief, while the Journalist plied us with her favorite self-help books on the subject of mental fluidity—more than fifty of them by midweek. Even the Silent Man joined in, although I can't recall his contribution.

By Thursday morning I'd had enough theoretical caregiving, and I let the group know I intended to visit our friend that night, despite the absence of invitation. No one objected, and several half-heartedly offered to accompany me. I believe they were all relieved not to have to go themselves.

Mrs. Hillyer answered the front door, and before I could apologize for my unannounced intrusion, she took my hand and led me with some urgency down the hall to the library. From behind the room's closed door I could hear what sounded like gunfire. There were shouts and explosions, too.

"He's in a right state tonight, he is," she told me. "Really, he's been like this all week, since dinner last. He's practically locked himself away with that infernal machine."

"His time machine?"

Mrs. Hillyer responded with a look of bewilderment and then doubt, as if she were suddenly reconsidering whether she should have let me into the house at all. "Time machine?" she said. "Is that what it's called?" She knocked twice on the door, and without waiting for a reply she turned the knob, opened the door, and pushed me into the room. Before I could say anything, she closed the door behind me.

The library was unusually cold, and mostly entirely dark. All the lamps were switched off, there was no fire in the hearth, and the room's only illumination came from a number of flatscreen computer monitors mounted to the wall where the bookcase had been. Their bright light made me squint in the darkness, and unsettling shadows flickered everywhere. It reminded me of something by the conceptual artist Nam June Paik—in fact, I think he had a piece called *TV Wall* built from a similar number of screens. This arrangement, however, was more like a flatscreen wall of horrors, with images of starships bursting into flames, soldiers raked by machine-gun fire, samurai swordsmen committing ritual suicide by disembowelment, zombies digging into flesh. All in high-definition.

Directly in front of this abominable fancy, in trembling silhouette, was seated the Time Traveler. When I stepped closer, I could see his hands were clasped around a game controller, his fingers a blur of motion over joystick and buttons, and I realized he was not simply an observer, but also an actor in the apocalyptic action on every screen. I took a step closer and spoke his name, but of course he didn't answer: he could scarcely hear me over the tumult of computer-animated misery—screeching tires, explosions, teeth ripping into wet flesh, all that wailing and crying. I took another step forward, careful to avoid the empty bottles scattered over the floor: mostly alcohol, I think. And cans of soda—something called Jolt? And the remains of packaged sandwiches and biscuits.

I called his name again, louder this time, but still received no answer. Finally I placed a hand on his shoulder. He jerked at my touch and looked up at me with a scowl, possibly intended for Watchett or Mrs. Hillyer. But when he recognized my face, he relaxed. He paused all the screens—which thankfully silenced them as well—and then dropped the controller and struggled to his feet. He embraced me as if we'd been apart for much longer than the seven days since I'd last seen him.

"I apologize for arriving unannounced," I began, "but I've been concerned. We've all been—"

He embraced me again and this time kissed me on the lips, and I could smell liquor on his breath. Then he sank back into his comfy chair, and his eyes returned to the ghastly entertainments before him. I pulled up a chair to face him as he fumbled around, searching for his controller.

"How are you?" I asked, but he didn't answer. I might almost have believed he'd forgotten I was there. I noticed then that the video game controller was on the floor tucked behind his feet, and I picked it up. Only then did he look at me again.

"Care for a drink?" he asked, and he reached over the far side of his chair and returned with an empty bottle of whisky. He held it out. "I'm afraid I'm out of glasses," he said, his voice barely a whisper. He proffered the bottle a second time, but this time noticed it was empty. He took a deep breath and then exhaled slowly, then let the bottle slip from his hand. It thudded on the carpet. Our eyes met briefly, and he reached for the controller in my hand. I let him take it from me.

He said: "I've made a breakthrough, you know."

16

The Multimedia Machine

HE LEANED BACK IN HIS CHAIR and set the controller on his lap. He took another deep breath, sighed. Then he ran both hands through his hair. I thought he might have been working up the strength—or the courage—to speak, but before he could begin, the library door opened and Watchett entered. He was carrying two bottles, a large Pellegrino and another whisky. He placed the water on the table between us and the whisky on the floor beside the comfy chair. His movements were both particular and exact, and he'd obviously performed this routine many times during the past week. He fetched two glasses from the cupboard above the desk, and the Time Traveler eyed Watchett as he filled both glasses with sparkling water. He pulled a lime from his pocket, and a small knife, and expertly quartered the fruit while holding it in his hand, adding a wedge to each drink. I expected the Time Traveler to protest or grumble, but instead he remained silent, picked up his glass, and drained it at once. Watchett refilled it with water.

I took this opportunity to examine my friend. He appeared pale; his cheeks, sunken; his eyes, red and puffy. Overall drawn and tired, and for the first time frail, older than his years.

Before Watchett withdrew, he placed a flat circular tin beside the bottle of Pellegrino. As soon as the door closed, the Time Traveler began:

"I realized," said he, "that I've been going about this the wrong way. Time travel is impossible."

I raised an eyebrow. That was not what I expected him to say, but I wasn't displeased. This sounded like progress.

He continued: "I have been reconsidering the epistemology of my researches—the very nature and scope of knowledge and justified belief, as well as the means of production of knowledge." He reached for the small tin and unscrewed its lid. "That sounds a bit like Marx, doesn't it? I'd rather it was more Groucho than Karl. I don't have much Groucho left in me." He placed both lid and tin back on the table, then took a sip of water. As he drank we looked upon one another, and to frailty and fatigue I added sorrow.

"None of my inventions have worked." He put down the glass. "The only way to travel through time is slowly, inexorably, and in the forward direction. Backward is impossible. I don't think it even makes sense."

"I agree," I said.

"And relativistic travel offers only the illusion of time travel, you understand. Different people may move *forward* through time at different speeds of life, but so what. It doesn't *change* anything. It's useless. Or at the very least it's useless to me."

He reached for the open tin and picked out a pink pastille, looked at it, then popped it into his mouth. He sucked on it for several moments. He appeared contemplative, but also a little bit vague; and when he resumed speaking, I felt as if he were talking to himself, more than to me.

"I can't save her, can I," he said, and it was not a question. He reached for another pastille. "Basically, I'm fucked."

I wanted to hug him, but I held back. I could tell this position was precarious; his realization, a porcelain teacup in a child's hand. If this was a breakthrough, I knew I had to proceed cautiously, do whatever I could to protect it, to move him towards acceptance; and if making acceptance, then a kind of peace.

He sank back into his comfy chair, and I watched as his eyes moved from one gruesome image to the next. He seemed hypnotized, and without affect; but I could see the magnetic hold the screens had over him.

"Still, you must agree—you must have no doubt—that it was the worst outcome possible. Any other would be preferred."

"You've said that before, but surely it was a relief for her, not to live in pain," I said.

"Of course."

"And surely it must be better to have a choice? For her to have decided when to end her life."

"Yes, although I bear responsibility for making the idea of suicide acceptable. I allowed it to be possible."

"Euthanasia isn't suicide. It's a mercy."

"Mercy!"

"And *everyone* dies. A plane crashes. A cancer spreads. A branch falls from a tree. It is always heartbreaking, an utter catastrophe. But to say that any other outcome for her would be preferred? It doesn't make sense."

He looked at me as if I were mad. "For her? I am not talking about *her*. No, it was the worst outcome for *me*. To see her suffer. To suffer her suffering. To want it to end—to want *her life* to end. Don't you understand? *I killed her.*"

He reached for the new bottle of whisky and unscrewed its top. Tears began to roll down his cheeks. He refilled his glass and—as he had done with the sparkling water—he finished the first pour in one drought, and then poured himself a second. He raised the glass, hand trembling.

"And if you were expecting something more from me tonight—" He shook his head, then took another drink. "Science, mind, heart, spirit—there's no way out. So if you think I invited you here to demonstrate some new invention, you are gravely mistaken."

I watched as he refilled his glass once more, then his gaze

returned to the horror show frozen in front of him. I considered pointing out that I had not in fact been invited at all, but I bit my tongue. He sipped his drink slowly and steadily until it was gone. I felt a terrible sympathy for my friend. I bowed my head. I'd come here to help, but I realized then that I had no idea what to do.

He placed the glass back on the table and pushed the small tin of pastilles towards me. I picked one out, then took a closer look at the lid. A psychedelic Peter Max–inspired graphic said "Pink Pony," and I realized my host was offering me a low-dose edible with fifteen milligrams of tetrahydrocannabinol, or THC. I put the candy back.

"At least," the Time Traveler was saying, "not of my own devising."

"I'm sorry. What?"

"I said I have no invention to show you."

"Right."

"At least not one of my own devising."

"Wait, what?"

"Perhaps I was not clear. I can't save Tamara, I can't rewrite history, but I may still save myself. Not with any of my inventions, of course—none of them have worked. But lo and behold—someone else has found a solution." He pointed towards the video wall. "There may be no objective externalized time travel, but it's clear that subjective internalized travel is not only possible, but inherent. In fact, it may be what sets us apart from the rest of creation." He waved his empty glass in the air. "But don't misunderstand me. I am not making a religious argument, for it doesn't matter if we are in this regard unique or not. I don't care."

"Here now," I objected, trying to regain what suddenly seemed like lost ground. "A moment ago you acknowledged that time travel is impossible. That other than the most banal interpretations, we are limited to our own time—and our own timeline. We're stuck; you said so yourself."

"Here, yes"—he continued to wave his glass in the air—

"in London, in Richmond, in the here and now." He banged his chest with his fist. "This mortal flesh, this body. The organs, the sinew, the very cells that comprise my being. My soul, too, for that matter. All of it. Whatever is here, whatever is me. Time travel: *impossible.*"

I nodded tentatively. I could feel the rug about to be pulled out from under my feet, and pull it he did:

"But *here* "—and this time he tapped the tumbler to his skull—"in my brain, escape is possible. We are, after all, just the sum of our senses. You will admit that, certainly."

"Well…."

"There is no getting over grief. I've said as much before. We tumble over the precipice and must say farewell to everything left behind. There is no negotiation. There is no climbing back. We cannot fly. The only thing to do is to fall. You understand, don't you, the philosophy of perception?"

For a moment I was speechless. And for a moment I wondered whether I wanted to have this conversation at all. But what else could I do?

I answered his query: "Do you mean the difference between our perception of objects and the objects themselves? That our perception is fundamentally idiosyncratic, mediated by mind?"

The Time Traveler laughed. "I hope you are not a naïve realist."

"Well," I parried, "I do believe in an external reality."

The Time Traveler wagged his finger at me. "Of course, but *that* is not the question."

"Then what is the question?"

"Whether our mind—our senses—trumps everything, regardless of external reality."

I thought about it for a moment. "'Reality is that which, once you stop believing in it, doesn't go away.'"

"Philip Dick! True enough, I suppose, but so what? Do you deny the internal reality of optical illusions? The obvious relativity of perceptual experience? Hallucinations? *Feelings?"*

"Yes, very well. The mind is the backstop. I will concede that. If all you're concerned about is an individual's experience, then the subjective, the internalized, constitutes a kind of reality."

The Time Traveler seemed satisfied with that response. He placed his glass on the table between us. He picked out another pastille and popped it into his mouth.

"So the solution—or the trick—is not to pick up and move the body through time; the trick—or the solution—is to change the mind. I'm sure our mutual friend the Psychologist—or the Therapist, or whatever he or she is called this week—would agree. Change your mind and the rest will follow. And that's what all this is for." He pointed to the wall of screens. "When one dream is lost, there are plenty of other dreams to take its place."

"But these aren't even dreams—they're nightmares!"

"How would you know? You, who can't even recognize the nightmare you're in today. You said it yourself. Everyone dies. A plane crashes. A cancer spreads. A chicken bone gets caught in the throat. And in the blink of an eye you lose everything. All times are end times. Forget those stories about *future* dystopias—you live in a dystopia *right now*. A world of endless and inevitable loss."

"Really, I don't think—"

"From God's lips to my ears, if I can open my eyes wide enough and let this video nasty *shit* spill in—well, I promise you it's like knocking back the smoothest scotch. Which reminds me...." He reacquired the bottle of whisky and this time skipped the glass entirely. He took two hasty gulps, then gestured towards the wall. "Look at all these stories, these waking dreams, these diabolic distractions. *Where has tomorrow gone?* Right here. Alternate worlds—I've got them all! The future, the past. 'All these worlds are yours except Europa.' Well, fuck Europa. She's been taken from Europa.

And if I can't live with her *right here*, I'll be damned if I don't find her somewhere else. Surely she's somewhere else— somewhere in here!"

He un-paused the center screen and the war game reanimated. Gunfire, explosions, screams of despair. *"And to be honest,"* he shouted over the din, *"I also like to blow things up!"* He wiped a sleeve across his wet cheek, and then un-paused the other screens.

"Please don't do this," I begged. "You don't have to do this. You don't have to give them Tamara. She's yours." I struggled to think of something better to say, but he wasn't listening. There was another explosion and more gunfire, tires screeching over dry roadway, teeth rending flesh.

"Oh shit shit shit!" he wailed—as a computer-generated curtain of blood dropped over the center screen. GAME OVER. The Time Traveler threw the controller across the room. "Watchett! Watchett! Get in here!"

I stood up and started towards the door.

"Watchett! For fuck's sake get in here!" he called again.

The door to the library opened and Watchett reappeared. This time he was cradling a large shopping bag in his arms. "Supplies," he whispered as he passed, and I edged my way out of the room. Mrs. Hillyer was waiting in the hallway. She pulled the door closed behind me.

"You see?" she said, her voice trembling. "All week. It's been like this—all week."

And again I didn't know what to say. I retreated down the hallway towards the front door. I could hear the Time Traveler shouting at Watchett even as I ran across the street.

17

The Time Traveler Returns

I HEARD NOTHING from the Time Traveler for two weeks, despite repeated entreaties via text, email, and even phone. Of course I was worried I might not hear from him at all after my last visit. I pictured him holed up in the library; growing increasingly gaunt and pale and agitated and angry and depressed; living off an endless resupply of junk food and cola and whisky; accepting—or acquiescing with prejudice—to the Fates; unable to face the world; unable to face future, past, or present; taking advantage of the generosity of his housekeepers; and slowly sinking into the quicksand of the internet and video games. But I was worried also about my own response to his condition, for it took several days before I worked up the courage to send that first message, and that was instead of my visiting him directly—storming the house if need be—to make sure he was alive and well and out of danger. So I was both surprised and relieved when a text arrived on Thursday morning, inviting us all to Richmond that evening. The message gave no indication of his previous distress: it was polite and engaging, witty, forthright, and earnest; and much closer in word and spirit to the manner of invitation we would have received a year ago, before his fiancée Tamara's death, before he began his unfortunate descent into the study of time travel, and before we'd seen him fail, time and again, in the construction of various mechanisms and devices that would enable his mad wanderlust through what he'd called the fourth dimension.

The surprising rehabilitation of character extended to his

abode as well. I had worried that upon arriving that evening I'd find the place a shambles, that the deplorable state of the library I'd witnessed two weeks before would have spread— like a noxious weed or mold—throughout the entire house. But nothing was further from the truth. His home was neat and tidy: unsoiled, unmarked, and altogether hospitable. There were no exposed cables nor wormy ductwork, no unsealed crates, no casually discarded fast-food wrappers, and not a single computer screen (streaming violence or otherwise). This is not to say the house had returned to normal, for it was apparent as soon as I entered the front hallway that this usually solemn home had been transformed into a place of celebration. There were helium balloons everywhere, of differing size, shape, and color; twisted festoons depending in lazy arcs above the entries to the drawing room and library; calligraphic signs that read "Welcome!" or "Congratulations!"; and a multitude of sweet blossoms and bouquets decorating the small tables along the passageway. Lively music—bossa nova, I think— was coming from speakers hidden in the walls, and when I arrived the house was packed with not only guests but revelers, young and old, many of whom I did not recognize. This was in fact not a dinner we'd been invited to, but a party.

The Provincial Mayor was in the library, dressed in the regal attire befitting his position in the metropolitan county of the West Midlands. Filby was there, too, standing by the fire warming his hands. (He must have arrived shortly before I did: the evening was cold and the forecast was more snow.) The Very Young Woman was sitting on the arm of a Victorian easy-chair sipping a cocktail, her free arm draped lazily over the shoulder of the seated Silent Man, who seemed pleased as her fingers began twirling his golden locks. The Psychologist (or perhaps it was the Therapist?) and the Medical Man (or the Physician?) stood off to the side, whispering back and forth. I wondered if their conversation concerned my previous report about our host, or if it were lighter in subject: perhaps the election of the new PM (and our first Trump). Meanwhile, the Electrician had climbed up on a wobbly chair beside the fireplace, stretching her long arms towards the dangling tether of a red balloon that had floated to the ceiling. The Contractor stood in front of her, arms wrapped all the way around the Electrician's waist to keep her from falling, cheek pressed against her hip. "Almost there," the Electrician gasped, "...almost there." The Frenchman—beret in one hand, e-cigarette in the other—was standing beside the Debutante, a heavy girl with a dramatic décolletage who kept touching her own bottom as if to reconfirm its existence. Carafes of wine, both red and white, and plates of crudités and cold cuts and cheese, were placed on the several hexagonal tables scattered about the room, and bottles of champagne stood like soldiers beside a pyramid of crystal flutes on the sideboard. The Editor, the Writer, and the Rabbi stood together near the bookshelves; and the Bishop slouched near the fire, splitting his attention between a glass of wine and the exposed belly of the Electrician as her silk shirt kept rising and falling as she stretched for the wayward balloon. The Prisoner was holding hands with the Software Developer, the Realtor was dancing by himself, and three Hippies near the door were huddled over a spliff, trying to light up. I recognized the Chancellor, the Mortician, the Striker, and the Zoologist.

I moved towards the bar just as the music stopped and a bell chimed three times over the house's speaker system. A voice I did not recognize requested that everyone gather in the library for a special announcement. Hillyer appeared then, at the library's entrance, carrying in several additional straight-back chairs, and Mrs. Watchett followed with another. She looked particularly severe, and carelessly dropped the chair in front of the portly Philatelist. Revelers from other parts of the house began to arrive—I recognized the Dietician, the Midwife, the Policeman, the Firefighter, the Respiratory Therapist, the Anti-vivisectionist—and both Mrs. Watchett and Hillyer had to push against the current to make their way back out of the room.

"I say!" I called to the Medical Man. "I'm not sure we'll all fit!"

More guests flowed into the room, and I found myself pressed against the sideboard, next to the Debutante and the Frenchman, and several newcomers including the Philosopher, the Equestrian, and the Graphic Designer. I don't think the library had ever been so completely overrun, and I soon found myself looking over a sea of heads. I picked out the Meteorologist, the Ophthalmologist, the Snake Milker, and the Professional Sleeper. There was a commotion near the door, and I noticed one of the guests— otherwise hidden within a swell of new arrivals—had raised his hand into the air. The crowd parted around it, and I realized the wiggling fingers belonged to our host. He pushed his way to the front of the room, taking a position before the fireplace. He began to speak, but stopped, realizing perhaps that he was still invisible to too many in the room. He reached for the hand of the Electrician and traded places with her upon the rickety chair. (The Contractor seemed momentarily disappointed at the change of circumstance, and then gamely wrapped his arms around the legs of our host and pressed his cheek to his thigh, holding him safely in place.) After an interval our host bid us all to sit, which was just one of many improbabilities the Time Traveler had shared with us over the past year, and so the vast majority continued to stand, perforce, shoulder to shoulder in the tight confines of the room.

"Uhra," he said into the air, "raise the lights and ask Mrs. Watchett to prepare dessert." The red eye of the panopticon that dangled from the ceiling twisted like a snake, then responded by blinking twice, and an artificial voice I recognized as our host's digital housekeeper acknowledged the request over the library's speakers.

The Time Traveler took a moment to regard his audience. If he was unsettled at all by the size of the gathering he did not show it. He was dressed casually, but stylishly, a simple grey duster over a white t-shirt and jeans, and he seemed radiant and happy, and neither dissipated nor drunk, and unlike I'd seen him for many months. His appearance wasn't preternatural: he did not look unscathed by his previous experiences. But at the very least the severe depression that had seemed to haunt him two weeks earlier had vanished. The Bishop handed the Time Traveler a glass of champagne—it had been passed hand to hand from the back of the room—and he raised the flute into the air.

"My friends, it is good to have you all here together. I know many of you are appearing for the first time—at least canonically—and I apologize for that. Kill your darlings, they say. But you're here now at last." He let his gaze sweep the room. A few more stragglers were arriving—the Oceanographer, the Poet, the Imam, the Gambler—but when he caught my eye he winked. "It has been a consequential year," he continued, "both the best and worst of times, and I've invited you all to my home this evening to share an epiphany I've had concerning the block universe theory of time…."

There were undisguised moans and groans from round the room. Several people muttered "Not again" or "Please, no." The Psychologist, pressed now beside me, shook her head and sighed. But our host wagged a finger at us all.

"Now, now—there's no need to despair! This will be the last time I expound on such recondite matters. And I promise not to bore you with details."

The Time Traveler took a sip of champagne, then with his free hand reached into an inner pocket of his jacket and pulled out a thin rectangular object. He raised it into the air.

"This," he said, "is my latest invention and the culmination of my work. I call it a literal manifestation of the eternal block model of time, and it is the device I use—have *already* used—to travel backward and forward and sideways in time."

He took another sip of champagne and then held out his newest prototype for all of us to see.

It was a paperback book.

18

The Timeless Machine

AND THEN the Time Traveler (for so it will be convenient to speak of him) raised his glass again. His grey eyes shone and twinkled, and his face was flushed and animated. The fire burned brightly, and the soft radiance of the incandescent lights from the wall sconces caught the champagne bubbles that flashed and passed in his glass. He handed the book to the Psychologist and told her to pass it round, and then the Time Traveler began the evening's recitation:

"There are two ways to think about time. There is presentism, according to which only the present exists. That is, there is no such thing as past or future, and time travel is impossible because there is nowhere to go. There's no there there—or rather no *when*."

There were a few titters around the room.

"A second way to think about time is that the past, present, and future exist. One example of this is called the eternal block view, in which all of spacetime is envisioned as one giant four-dimensional block. Past, present, and future co-exist, unchanging, and it is just our consciousness that moves in one direction through this block, along the axis of time. Everything that has happened, and everything that will happen, is already there; and although we experience a kind of presentism—we *feel* as if we are living in the present and that time passes—it's just an illusion."

"Just like my last paycheck!" exclaimed the Pastry Chef. The Accountant poked him in the ribs with a *shush*.

"There are of course block models of greater complexity. There's the growing block model in which the past and present exist while the future does not. As time passes, more of the world comes into being; therefore, the block universe is said to be growing. There's another model where the block is actually doughnut-shaped, a solid four-dimensional torus, and the present—or rather our experience of it—is actually an annihilation-creation wave moving around this doughnut, both destroying and re-creating time as it goes. One of the interesting features of this model is that when we look far into the past, we're just following the curve of the doughnut all the way round, and the Big Bang we see is actually the annihilation-creation we're experiencing in the present. Of course you'd think that would mean the Big Bang is a fixed distance from the present, and that it never recedes in time; however, the size of the doughnut is actually expanding—"

The Time Traveler looked round the room and saw eyes wide, glazed, and half-closed.

"But I digress. Let me return to this evening's concern. It's become clear to me over the course of my researches that time travel (as I've imagined it) is impossible. Whether we live in a present-only or block-model universe, you—the present you—cannot move forward and backward in time. You cannot change the past or alter the course of the future. Your mistakes cannot be undone, you cannot save the dead. Everything that *is*, *has been*, or *will be*—already exists."

"Hear! Hear!" Filby declared. "Now you're talking sense!"

The Time Traveler raised a hand. "Tamara became ill. She decided to die. And I helped her to kill herself. That's the way it will always be."

"Are you a fatalist, then?" demanded the Judge. "Everything is predetermined?"

"What is, is. We've got to accept it."

"A fatalist, then," confirmed the Gigolo.

"But there is a loophole. I accept that 'what is, is,' but that 'is' is richer than I once thought. In fact, our friend the doctor figured it before I did. I just wasn't ready to listen. For even if we can't rewrite history, we can rewrite ourselves." He tapped his temple as he had done two weeks before. "In here, in our head."

"I knew it!" the Medical Man bellowed. "Make-believe!"

"So I thought as well—at first. I went looking for Tamara in the dreams of others. Dreams of other worlds and other times. I let myself get lost in the violent doldrums of other people's stories, in superficial video games and social media. But of course she wasn't there—why would she be? Others' dreams are not my dreams."

"I hope never to see you in that state again," I said.

The Time Traveler met my eyes and then nodded. He took another drink. I could tell that simply speaking of these things had a terrible impact on him. "Eventually even her memory began to fade, overwritten by the distractions, the fancies, of others. I lost her in increments: her hair, her eyes, her voice, her touch—until she nearly disappeared. I think, my friend, if you had not visited me, I would have remained mesmerized, and she would have been wholly lost to me. You helped me realize my mistake. You were right. She was *my* Tamara, and the only way I might conjure her is through my own imagination. To remember her, everything about her, to dream her back to life, detail by detail, to make her as real as any of you."

"Dream her back to life? How——?" the Cinematographer began, but the Time Traveler cut her off.

"There is a rich history of using the imagination to permute reality and to conjure ideas into being—from summoning tutelary demons in the Western mystery tradition to the Haitian reanimation of a corpse, from cabalist litanies to blood and incense, from Borges to the *Witches of Eastwick*. I knew the mechanism that I needed must touch upon physics as well as the arts, track both pneuma and psyche, and present a shadow to reality. Of course, you already know what I found."

The Time Traveler raised a finger into the air. "Think of all of time as a book. It is in fact the perfect representation of the block model. The past and future are already written, and the present moment is what you are reading *right now*."

At this point he stepped down off the chair and approached the Very Young Woman, who was paging through the paperback.

"And time travel—is it possible? Well, of course!" The Time Traveler took the book from the woman and began to riffle its pages. He stopped several times to jab his lean finger to one passage and then another. "I can jump from past to future and back again, anywhere I want. I can jump from page to page in any order I wish. I can move my consciousness to whatever present I desire." Our host raised the book into the air.

"This, my friends, is the secret to time travel!"

"Well done!" said the Bishop.

"But it's not enough. Nothing can change this book. No matter how many times you read it. Past, present, future, it's already here and impossible to alter. As I've said: time, as we experience it, is an illusion. In that sense, this book is a mechanism without time. *It is a timeless machine*."

"Incredible!" said the Publisher. "And I work with books all the time."

"And yet this is the dilemma. A book is bound in the three dimensions of space and the fourth dimension of time. It's a singular artifact, even if copied, and constrained in alternate space. So how do I find room in here to bring her back? How can this mechanism hold enough imagination?"

"It seems you've set another impossible task before yourself," said the Psychologist.

The Time Traveler by this point had made his way to the sideboard. He shook hands with the Nude Model and then refilled his glass with champagne. "Yes, well, the answer turns out to be quite simple. Don't fight your constraints. Find a way around them. Move perpendicular to those axes. Forget the four dimensions of space and time. Find another direction. And that's exactly what I've done. That's why we are celebrating tonight—because the riddle is solved. The solution to Tamara's return is inside this book, and before the end of tonight she will walk through the front door!"

There were an equal number of gasps and groans around the library. He tossed me the paperback. I fumbled it for a moment and then flipped it over. It was called *The Timeless Machine*, and on its cover was a picture of a woman encircled by a number of stars. There were murmurs around the room as I studied the book, then opened it and turned to the table of contents. I read the names of the first few chapters: The Dinnertime Machine, The Altimeter Machine, The Septime Machine, The Pastime Machine, The Antimere Machine, The Ragtime Machine….

"The Dinnertime Machine?" I queried.

"The right combination of foods can speed or slow the metabolism. All you need to do is regulate the heartbeat—the master timekeeper—and one might be able to travel forward and backward in time."

"The Altimeter Machine?"

"A variant on special relativity—the effect of mass and acceleration on spacetime is analogous to the variability of gravity as it's reflected in altitude. Unfortunately, it requires access to a supersonic jet, and an iron stomach."

"The Pastime Machine?"

"The complement to the Half-time Machine. One applies tachyons—particles that can travel no *slower* than the speed of light—to special relativity. Unfortunately, the mechanism allows only retrograde movement in time."

"This is senseless," I said. "None of these methods can possibly work."

The Psychologist grabbed the book from me, looked down the list.

"The Ragtime Machine?" she asked.

"There is a kind of cross-rhythm hidden in the temporal shadow of every method used for the measurement of time—whether water clocks, spring clocks, sundials, mechanical clocks, quartz clocks. It's a pause, a silent beat, an absence of tempo, that reveals the localized shape of spacetime." The Time Traveler touched the Psychologist's cheek. "Damn. I should have changed the color of your skin, too."

"What's this all about?" the Medical Man interjected. "Did you write this book?"

The Time Traveler held up his hands. "Look at these fingers! Worn to the nub at the keyboard these past two weeks. I was obsessed. 'The moving finger writes; and, having writ, moves on....'"

The evening's guests began to chatter again amongst themselves, and the Psychologist returned the book to me. I flipped towards the back and skimmed the final chapter. It was called "The Timeless Machine." The Psychologist began to say something, but I waved her off. I couldn't believe what I was reading. Immediately, I raised my voice. I called for silence. When the room finally quieted, I read aloud what I had found:

> *He tossed me the paperback. I fumbled it for a moment and then flipped it over. It was called* The Timeless Machine *and on its cover was a picture of a young man encircled by a number of moons. There were murmurs around the room as I studied the book, then opened it and turned to the table of contents. I read the names of the first few chapters: The Wartime Machine, The Peacetime Machine, The Ofttimes Machine, The Fluxus Machine, The Timekeeping Machine, The Multimember Machine....*

"Why, this is us!" I exclaimed. "This is what is happening now, this very moment. How did you—?"

The Time Traveler took the book from me. "Don't you see? I didn't have to identify *a priori* the right way to bring her back, not if I can try them all, not if I can explore every possibility *right here* until I find the one that works."

"Recursion," I said. "You've written a recursive book. It's a story within a story, where each story is slightly different, and you're the outer narrator."

The Time Traveler nodded. "This book looks thin—and in space and time it is—but it's got a back door, a secret passage that tunnels on and on. You might call it *The Tome Machine*, thick enough to bean into insensibility the most hard-headed gentleman scientist!" He laughed. "Don't you see? I've contrived to write a book that never ends, whose structure is iterative. A book that is finite in pages but infinite in length, that extends into forever but is also instantaneous. A book whose single purpose is to find a way to return Tamara to the real world, by testing every possible path! And if you believe there is a solution—*even just one solution*—the riddle is solved! Somewhere deep in this book, in this rectangular ruin, in this *mise en abyme*, is the answer to her resurrection. It's unequivocal. Before the last word is read, she will return. You'll see!"

The Time Traveler tossed the book to the Provincial Mayor and then made his way towards the door, just as Mrs. Watchett re-entered the room carrying a tray of petit fours and croissants. Hillyer followed close behind with two large urns of coffee.

"Just desserts—at last! Uhra," our host called into the air. "Music, maestro, please!"

Overhead the red eye of the panopticon responded by blinking twice. The lights dimmed and the music started again—nu jazz, this time—and having now heard the meat of the evening's sermon, the revelers were ready for their pudding. Guests surrounded the trays of pastries, refilled their glasses, and began to gossip and chitter-chatter. The Flautist shared her champagne with the Copyeditor, the Accountant embraced the Actress, and the dancing Realtor grabbed the hand of the German Minimalist. As the evening's revelry resumed, the Time Traveler slipped out the library's entrance. I caught the eye of the Very Young Woman and together we pushed through the partygoers to follow our host. When we reached the door we discovered the Psychologist and the Medical Man had the same idea.

"The laboratory?" I suggested, and the four of us made our way down the passage. The door was open and we found our host inside, already seated at a workbench, pulling paperbacks off a large stack and signing them. The lab was as tidy as the rest of the house, but undecorated save a mosaic of photographs on one of the walls. The pictures were all of our host's fiancée.

The Time Traveler looked up. "You have more questions?"

"I feel confused," I said. "As if this has all been a sham, or fiction. Was it all a dream?" I gestured to the tall stacks of paperbacks on the workbench, all copies of *The Timeless Machine*. "Is this really the culmination of your work?"

"I've succeeded at last. In that sense it is both the beginning and ending."

"I feel confused, too," said the Very Young Woman. "Have you been playing with us? It's all exceptionally Zen. Are we all One? Am I nothing more than a fiction to you?"

"Of course not!"

The Medical Man stepped forward. "So you've reached a kind of acceptance, then? You've honestly given up on time travel—on changing the past?"

"I've told you, changing the past—it's impossible." He picked up a signed copy of the book from the stack. "It's already written, you see. There is no way to change any of it, from this moment back to our first dinner together. I can't just have Filby turn up on page 57 in a clown's costume. You may check, but you'll see it's impossible."

"And yet you believe Tamara will return?"

The Time Traveler took a deep breath. "Don't be astonished to find that my wounds have healed." He handed the signed copy of the book to the Medical Man, then turned to contemplate the mosaic of photographs on the wall. "Sometimes it seems as if our lives are stories without an author, doesn't it? Our narratives, hopeless and entangled, inconsistent, seemingly with no sense. And yet, our lives are stories filled with authors. Each of us—all of us. So many authors, telling our stories. Doesn't it make you wonder why?"

"But surely they're not real. That's the whole point, isn't it. Like myths. Stories are stories," the Medical Man said. "I *suppose* they might help you with your grief—"

"My grief?" The Time Traveler picked up another copy of his book, signed it, and then handed it to the Psychologist. "I told you already. Grief is timeless. Which is why this—my timeless machine—is the only solution. It's the only wiggle room we've got. It's time travel without time. It's infinite possibility. It's invention crossed with forever. The last chapter of each book opens into the next, and the next, and the next—like those innumerable turtles that carry the world on their backs. Because there is no way forward except inward. Deeper into ourselves, into our stories. Don't you understand? Infinite regress is required because *it's grief all the way down.*"

I was about to speak, to question his logic—or at least the application of what I thought was his wildest theory yet—when there came a sudden noise from down the hallway: a startling cry, followed by a rising clamor. The Time Traveler jumped to his feet. His grey eyes shone and twinkled once more, and his lips curled into a curious smirk.

"She's here," he said. "She's back."

This time will not come again.
The magic word in life is *then*.
And *then*, and *then*, and *then*....

— Ekkel Church, "Clocked"

Mark Malamud is an inventor, poet, and puzzle-maker. His collection of short stories, *The Gymnasium*, established the idea of literary taxidermy. He is the co-editor of *A Pocketful of Fish*, an omnibus of poetry by Choo 3T Fish. He lives in the Pacific Northwest.

Pleasure to Burn

An anthology of literary taxidermy based on the first and last lines of *Fahrenheit 451* by Ray Bradbury. Award-winning stories from the 2019 Literary Taxidermy Short Story Competition.

On the Orient Express

By altering an event early in Christie's mystery—this time there is no murder—the remaining text must adjust to accommodate the absence of the crime. The result is a transformation of the original novel into something entirely different: an expression of redemption rather than of revenge. A re-novel by Mark Malamud.

A Pocketful of Fish

A seaworthy celebration of dubious poetry, this omnibus brings together three previously published volumes: *Swimming through the Darkness* (1974), *Roe Roe Roe Your Boat* (1978), and *Will You Hold My Breath* (1994). Poetry by Choo 3T Fish, recipient of the National Poetry Award in 1974 and the Boating Association *Truite d'Or* in 1980.

The Gymnasium

Nineteen tales of melancholy and wonder created by "re-stuffing" what goes in between the opening and closing lines of classic works by Milan Kundera, Philip K. Dick, Thomas Wolfe, Ian Fleming, and others. The inspiration for the Literary Taxidermy Short Story Competition. Short stories by Mark Malamud.

www.regulus.press